The Marshal from Deadwood

The Marshal from Deadwood

TODHUNTER BALLARD *1903-*

Sagebrush
Large Print Westerns

Library of Con~~gress Cataloging in Publication Data~~

38212002598792
Main Adult Large Print
Ballard, Todhunte~~r~~ Ballard, Todhunter, 1903-
The marshal fr The marshal from Deadwood
  p.   cm.   [text (large print)] JAN 9 8
ISBN 1-57490
  1. Large type books. 1. Title.
[PS3503.A5575M37   1997]
813'.54--dc21   97-40245
                                                    CIP

Cataloguing in Publication Data is available from
the British Library and the National Library of Australia.

Sagebrush Large Print Westerns are published in the United States
and Canada by Thomas T. Beeler, Publisher, Box 659,
Hampton Falls, New Hampshire 03844-0659. ISBN 1-57490-094-3

Published in the United Kingdom, Eire, and the Republic of South
Africa by Isis Publishing Ltd, 7 Centremead, Osney Mead, Oxford
OX2 0ES England. ISBN 0-7531-5831-0

Published in Australia and New Zealand by Australian Large Print
Audio & Video Pty Ltd, 17 Mohr Street, Tullamarine, Victoria, 3043,
Australia. ISBN 1-86340-741-3

Manufactured in the United States of America by BookCrafters, Inc.

The Marshal from Deadwood

CHAPTER 1

NEITHER LESTER HOE NOR THE DRIVER HAD SPOKEN IN twenty miles. It was too cold for talk They rode shoulder to shoulder on the swaying seat, their knees under a worn buffalo robe, their upper bodies screened from the bitter downdraft by fleece-lined coats whose wide collars were turned up, almost to the level of their hat brims.

It was the middle of July, but snow still lingered in the Colorado high country, and the stream below the twisting road ran bank-full edged with wafer ice, its roar blending with the creak of the swaying vehicle and the clink of their horses' shoes on the scarred rocks of the rising trail.

A distant moon, shafting its rays through the clumps of aspen and pole pine which studded the canyon sides, threw the men into sharp relief of shadowed contour.

The driver was near middle age, his cheeks protected from the chill by a mat of heavy, black, curly beard. Only his nose showed, bulbous and veined. The eyes were in deep shadow beneath the low-drawn hat.

Lester Hoe buried his chin as deep as possible in the protecting collar. His neckerchief was raised and bound about his ears against the cold, and his dark eyes were intent on the winding road ahead.

It ran up before them like a tortured snake as they climbed, hugging the jutting, timber-covered boulders, searching for space between the canyon wall and the raging stream, crisscrossing the creek, sometimes on crude bridges, logs spiked to stringers that groaned beneath the weight of the heavy coach as the wheels

1

bumped across the corduroy surface, smoothed only slightly by its layer of sand and mud.

At other times they forded, the big wheels crushing the border ice, plowing hub deep in the rushing water, the straining six horses lunging into their collars to lift their burden up the steepness of the far bank. Only then did the driver break his silence to swear encouragement at his fighting team.

Hoe never so much as turned his head. He was a big man, without appearing either tall or heavy, his body a series of flat planes running down from his wide shoulders across his narrow flanks to powerful legs; but now he looked hunchbacked and deformed as he bent nearly together, trying to conserve his warmth against the beating of the downwind.

Only a fool would ride a coach top on a night like this if there were room inside, but the round body of the swaying stage held a preacher, his complaining wife and three small fussy girls. Hoe had stood their company to Bronson's Crossing, but then had joined the driver, unable to stomach the woman's constant laments.

It was well after midnight before the canyon's grade slackened as it widened into a grassed meadow and they pulled up before the squared log walls of Teal's White Boar's Head Inn.

The hostlers came running to change the team. The driver lifted his stiffened joints down over the wheel and, opening the coach door, muttered to the dark interior: "Twenty-minute stop. Coffee and sandwiches in the front room." Then, as if he owed nothing further to his passengers' comfort, he headed for the taproom door at the side of the building.

Hoe sat unmoving, watching the preacher alight, followed by his spare, unattractive wife, who herded the

2

three small children before her like a fussy hen, complaining at every step.

"You weren't content with the church in Baltimore. It was too easy, you said. You could only serve God properly in these miserable mountains. Do you think He is deaf to prayers said beside a comfortable fire?"

The man's voice had the tone of thunder. "Silence, woman! Cease to blaspheme before your innocent children."

They were still arguing as the station's heavy door swung shut behind them and cut off the sound. Lester Hoe stood up slowly. He stretched, grinning to himself. Even men of God, it seemed, sometimes had trouble with their women. With a natural grace which even stiffened muscles could not defeat, he dropped easily to the ground and followed the driver's steps to the taproom.

Teal was an Englishman. Rumor had it that his family gladly paid him well to stay as far as possible from the manor where he had been born. A sandy man with the receding chin and slightly curved nose which marked the Saxon strain, he stood behind his crude bar, two planks supported by beer kegs, and served the driver, and then lifted an eyebrow toward Hoe.

"Whiskey." Hoe thought it useless to specify the brand and was surprised when Teal produced a bottle plainly marked as Scotch. Not until he tasted his drink did he realize it had been refilled with forty-rod.

The Englishman grinned at the face he made. It was one of Teal's jokes, along with the taproom sign and the crudely drawn white boar's head on the wall behind the bar.

"Bit of old England, what?"

Hoe did not answer. The raw alcohol was coursing

3

down through his empty stomach, shocking it into warmth. The driver wiped his bearded lips with the back of his none-too-clean hand.

"I swear to God I'm going to quit this run before I freeze or break my fool neck. I'd have quit before, but the Queen threatens to shoot me if I stop."

"She will, too." It was Teal. He refilled Hoe's empty glass, saying, "Compliments of the house." His lips under the edge of the sandy mustache were soft and mobile, like a woman's. "Heading for Two Mile, stranger?"

"If that's where the stage goes."

"She goes where the trail goes. Runs up the gulch to the town and then smack into the mountain. Heard once Seldom Seen McCrakken claimed he climbed out the other end with a bear chasing him, but I hardly believe it. Seldom Seen has never been known to tell the truth."

Lester Hoe did not answer, and Lord Teal, as he was known to everyone in that part of the territory, decided he was unsociable and that the free drink had been wasted.

The door at the rear of the shedlike bar created a diversion by being pushed open, and a small man appeared. He took four steps into the room, stopped, his narrow, ferret's face suddenly gaining a look of consternation. "Les Hoe."

Teal did not hear. He was bent double behind the bar, refilling his bottle, but Hoe stiffened and turned swiftly, his right hand sweeping back the skirt of his coat to expose the Colt in its worn holster.

He stopped thus, not drawing the gun, for the small man had taken a retreating step, and he straightened slowly. "I wondered where you'd been hiding, Sawyer."

The small man ran a nervous tongue around the dry

4

circle of his lips, and his voice was jumpy, low. "This ain't Deadwood, and you're not marshal here. Besides I ain't done a thing since I come into this country, not a single thing."

A smile lighted Hoe's dark, almost Indian face, and a devil sparked his dark eyes, a devil of mockery. "I'll bet you haven't, including work."

Teal straightened, the bottle full. The driver was staring. Hoe's attention remained centered on the small man. "You are a thief, a liar and a murderer and I meant what I told you in Dakota. Keep out of my way. I don't care that the judge turned you loose. You should have hanged."

Sawyer teetered on one foot, then the other. There was a gun in his belt and a look of hungry eagerness in his close-set eyes. Both Teal and the watching driver expected him to draw. He didn't. The instant when he might have mustered the courage passed, and he turned, scuttling for the safety of the outside darkness like a pack rat disturbed in an abandoned cabin.

The door slammed. Teal drew a long, slow breath. "First time I ever saw Booze Sawyer back down from anyone."

The stage driver grunted, "First time you ever saw him meet Les Hoe."

Teal had been below the counter when Sawyer had first gasped the name and had not heard it, but he caught it now. "Marshal of Deadwood." He studied Les Hoe with frank curiosity. "Heard of you. Thought you'd be older."

Hoe said nothing.

"Heard you were coming. Heard the Queen had sent for you. Knew your brother Marc. Didn't like him. Damn bully." His pale-blue eyes dared Hoe to resent the

5

words.

Hoe said calmly, "Didn't like him either."

The Englishman's sly grin lifted one corner of his sandy mustache. "Maybe I'll like you. Don't like most gunmen. Bunch of bouncers if you ask me." He poured another drink. "Sorry it's so bad. Not fit for a gentleman, you know, but then, most of my customers aren't gentlemen."

Les grinned and downed the drink. He found himself liking Teal and was surprised. He was not a man who made friends easily.

"You're going to take Marc's place?"

"We'll see."

"If the Queen says you will, you will. Never saw as determined a woman. Named her the Queen, I did, after Old Vic. Same stubborn, willful female. Breaks every man who won't dance to her music. Reason I'm here. Ran me out of Two Mile, she did. Threatened to whip me on the street. Man can't fight a woman, now can he?"

Les chuckled at the picture the words built in his mind. He could visualize Grandmère standing in the middle of the street, facing this tall Englishman, threatening him with her ox whip.

"I guess not," he said. "At least, no one has ever licked her yet.

CHAPTER 2

THE WOMAN WAS EXACTLY FIVE FEET TALL. HER FACE was oval and still smooth, with hardly a wrinkle despite her sixty-five years.

In her youth she had possessed beauty such as is

6

given few women to enjoy, and she still had a stately comeliness marred only by the small lines which radiated dike tiny threads of spider web from the corners of her black eyes.

Her jet hair, braided and wound in a sleek coronet, showed only the slightest trace of gray and gave inches to her appearance, and her dress with its deep bustle was gray serge, beneath a lace bosom which continued into a ribbed collar high about her throat.

She stood in her sitting room on the top story of Two Mile House and considered her youngest grandson, her eyes hard, protruding, as if her collar were fastened too tight.

"Took you long enough to come." Even after fifty years a slight trace of her native Cajun lingered in her pronunciation. "I was afraid you'd refuse to come."

"I almost did." Hoe crossed to settle himself on the horsehair sofa. The room's furnishings were rich in dark, heavy mahogany. Its weight reminded him of the wicked trail, the stretching grades up which he had so recently ridden, and his admiration grew for the teamsters who had freighted it and the mining machinery and all the building materials for the town.

Man, he thought, was unstoppable when fortune called. There was no more remote camp in Colorado than Two Mile, no richer camp, no larger one. Twenty thousand people huddled in this barren gulch, laboring in the huge mines which had already driven their tunnels miles into the bitter earth of Rock Mountain, and everything they ate, wore or drank came up the impossible road by wagon.

"You're stubborn," she said. She walked around him with the arrogant curiosity of a small Napoleon. "Like your father, only he was a fool along with being

7

stubborn. Why did he have to go to war, to get himself killed for Jeff Davis and the other big planters? What did they ever do for us?"

It was an old lament which Hoe had heard all during his childhood, and he made no answer. Instead he sat waiting, wondering why she had sent for him.

"Are you a fool, too, wearing that gun, strutting like a peacock so that every tough in the country will want to try to outshoot you?"

He said mildly, "Someone has to be a peace officer." He still could not understand why she had called him, unless she wanted him to avenge Marc's death. But he should have known it was fruitless to argue with her. None of them had ever succeeded, with the possible exception of Marc, and Marc had been very like her.

She was a tyrant, brooking no opposition, forcing others to her will, contemptuous of their desires or opinions. Perhaps she had been right, for she had accomplished the impossible.

Coming West with four grandchildren, the oldest, Marc, only fifteen when they started, she had accumulated vast wealth in a business usually reserved for men—mining. It was no secret how she had accomplished this. She had opened a small store in Two Mile when the struggling camp had contained less than three hundred people. Somehow she had gained the trust of the Denver wholesalers and in return had grubstaked every prospector who approached her.

In another camp she might have gone bankrupt, but Two Mile stood at the head of Lost Horse Gulch, which gouged its narrow slit into the bald side of Rock Mountain, and the center of the mountain seemed made of gold.

Not one, but a full dozen, of the men she had staked

8

struck it, with the result that she owned a sizable interest in every paying property but one in the camp.

Most of her early partners had sold out, but Marie Hoe had held her stock, buying more, combining the mines with the help of Eastern financiers until her Consolidated Rock Mining Company ran the district.

Many people wondered why his grandmother bad not taken her millions and headed for Denver, for the East, or even for Europe, as so many of the mining titans were doing, but although he had not seen her for six years, Lester Hoe knew what force held her in these hills. It was her hate for Asa Clayborne. This hate had brought her West in the first place, had made her trail Clayborne from one town to the next, and Les would have bet every double eagle in his belt that Clayborne was in Two Mile, otherwise Marie Hoe would not have stayed, despite her riches.

"A peace officer, a marshal." Her slightly shrill voice was edged with contempt. "Any ragtail who can handle a gun could do your job."

"Why do you care?"

She glared at him. "Why do you think I sent for you after the way you ran away from us in Denver?"

He had not run away. He had simply gotten himself a hostler's job in a Denver livery and refused to leave when the family had moved on to Two Mile. He had not taken the job because he loved horses, but because of a desperate need to escape Grandmère's domination and the family's Odyssey as Grandmère trailed Asa Clayborne, fired on by her burning hate.

That in the last ten years he had risen from hostler to one of the best-known marshals in the West was more due to accident than design. One evening he had saved the sheriff's life when the peace officer had been cornered in the livery by four drunken riders. In return he was made a deputy, and he had worn the star only six months when he broke the Coffee gang, killing three and putting two behind bars.

Wells Fargo had hired him. Later, still working for the express company, he had been sent to Deadwood, where that roaring camp's citizens' committee had begged him to tame the place.

Even if Grandmère had not written after Marc's murder, he would have moved on, for Deadwood was now fading fast, but he still was not sure why he had been summoned.

"I haven't the slightest idea why you wrote, unless you want me to hunt down Marc's murderer."

She said, "Marc's dead." There was no emotion in her voice, and he thought that in his memory she had never shown emotion for any of them. In fact, at times she had seemed to hate their existence. "Nothing you could do would bring him back, and the man who fired the bullet is dead. What I need is his brains. Neither Clint nor Raoul has them. I was hoping you'd developed some, now that you've grown up."

He watched her, trying to assess what her words might mean.

"Reports have it that you're tough, and that kind of reputation should help. But it takes more to run this town and my business than animal toughness. Raoul is soft. All he thinks about is women, and how fancy he looks in his clothes. Clint has a sly streak in him, and I don't trust sly men. That's why I sent, for you. My stock holdings are close to fifteen million shares. That makes me sound rich, but responsibility goes with power. How good are you when it comes to responsibility?"

Fifteen million shares. He could not help recalling the

three-room house on South Slough outside Cape Girardeau. There was nothing pleasant in his memories of the house or of the town, although as a small boy he had not been too conscious of the gulf that separated him and his brothers from the children of the people who lived on the hill.

He was in the third grade before he was forcibly made aware of the distinction. It was on his ninth birthday, and Grandmère had promised a party, the first he had ever had, and he dredged up the courage to invite Nell Clayborne. In those days Nell had been taffy-haired, with bright blue eyes, a tiny bubbling creature he had worshiped from afar.

He would never forget her answer. She had been disappointed, for she had loved parties. "I can't come," she told him. "My daddy doesn't want us playing with river trash."

River trash. Fifteen million shares in one of the richest mines in the West. It seemed incredible that Grandmère had amassed so much, that he, Les Hoe, could take over the management of her affairs. But would he actually take over? Marc, for all his ability, had been little more than an animated manikin subject to Grandmère's passing whim.

He watched the small woman, and she stared back at him, a hostility in her manner, as if she resented that he sat there alive while Marc was dead. He stood up slowly. "This is a new idea," he said. "The possibility of my taking Marc's place never entered my mind. Give me a little time to think."

Some of her old-time temper flashed at him. "Think, what's there to think about? A man should be able to make up his mind fast. Why did Marc have to die? Why couldn't it have been you?"

He did not answer. Nor did he look at her as he moved to the door, opened it and stepped into the hall. The hotel was by far the most impressive building in Two Mile. It reared an ungainly four stories above the west side of the narrow, winding main street. Behind it the canyon wall rose sharply. The rocky slope was less than fifteen feet away.

The builders had made a virtue of this, for instead of fire escapes they had built bridges from each story, so that it was possible to enter or leave the hotel without going anywhere near the lobby. The lobby itself was a work of art. The floor was tiled, the desk mahogany, and the deep-seated chairs leather upholstered. Les had no idea what Grandmère had spent on it, but he would not have been surprised had the sum run half a million.

He paused before the desk handing in his room key as he glanced at the throng of salesmen, mining men, and Eastern visitors who filled the place. The clerk smiled ingratiatingly, as if he knew Hoe was his future boss.

Hoe said, "Have you any idea where I might find my brothers?"

The clerk turned to the wall clock. It was fifteen minutes after nine. Les realized he had been with Grandmère for over an hour.

"I'd guess the bank. It opens at nine."

Hoe walked the lobby's length, stepped around a group of men arguing the price of mining stock, and went through the double doors to the porch which overlooked the seething street. Two Mile was very short of thoroughfares; three crooked streets, which climbed the eastern shoulder of the gulch in ascending steps, connected with each other by short side passageways so steep that it was a wonder the heavy wagons could be moved up their rutted inclines.

12

The resulting jam of ore wagons, delivery carts, freight wagons, and stages crept between the raised sidewalks, at times not seeming to move at all, the sweating drivers filling the air with their cacophony of curses.

Les Hoe had seen many boom camps, but had never seen such a jumble as this. The sidewalk was no better, and after he descended the three steps and turned up the slatted path, he was jostled constantly by the crowd, miners off shift, their rough clothes still stained from underground labor, men in business suits, a few riders in boots and Levi's, a sprinkling of Chinese and Indians, and women.

The number of women on the street told that Two Mile had passed the boom stage and was a permanent camp, for until mines got into regular production, few workers ever brought their families to new diggings.

The hotel stood at the corner of First and Park, the Rock Mountain Bank filled the next corner. Hoe had covered half of the block when he glanced through the window of a millinery shop and found he was looking directly into Nell Clayborne's blue eyes. Sight of her brought a physical shock, washing over him like the cold shiver evoked by a plunge into ice water.

He had known that her family must be in Two Mile, or Grandmère would not have remained. He had even considered the possibility of meeting her, but he still was not prepared for the effect that sight of her caused.

He had not seen her for ten years, not since he had been sixteen and Grandmère with her four charges had trailed the Claybornes into Dodge City. They had stayed in Dodge less than six months; then word reached Grandmère that Judge Clayborne was moving to Denver City and she had acted quickly, selling the small

13

restaurant she had opened, buying a wagon and mules, loading her grandsons as she always did when the trek westward resumed.

It was in Denver that Les had separated from his family, and he had not seen the girl there, but he recognized her instantly. He was about to move on when he realized that the recognition was mutual, and on impulse turned to the door.

There was a small sign on the window: *Nell Clayborne. Hats Made to Order.* He broke step, one question which had been in his mind answered. She was probably not yet married. Wives seldom used their maiden names.

It was a small place, sandwiched between a hardware store and butcher shop. There were four chairs against the south wall, a bit of carpet on the floor, a plain wooden counter bisecting the room midway back, and a workroom at the rear, screened by a curtain. On the counter were a dozen wooden hat stands, holding hats, some of them gay with feathers.

He spent only a single glance on the room, his eyes coming back to the girl. Her hair was still the color of warm taffy, parted in the middle, pulled back and wound in a long bun at the nape of her neck. She was quietly dressed, a black skirt with white, high-necked shirtwaist. Her face was oval, smooth yet mobile with expression, her lips full, and the eyes still the odd electric blue that had bothered him even as a child.

"Hello, Nell." Many times in the quiet of the night when he stood on dark corners or patrolled the streets of Deadwood, he had pictured this meeting and reviewed what he would say to her. but now that the instant was here, all the colorful phrases escaped him.

"Hello, Les." Her voice was no longer piping as it

had been in childhood, but it still lacked timber, seeming to come only from her throat, not her chest. "I heard you were coming." There was no smile on her lips, no real greeting in her eyes, only a wariness as if she were afraid of him.

Apparently everyone in Two Mile had been more certain he would answer his grandmother's summons than he had been, for up until the moment he had climbed aboard the stage in Denver he had been racked by hesitation.

"I won't ask if you're glad to see me."

"I'm not. I'm never glad to see any member of your family, and I know why you're here."

He gave her a slow, small boy's grin. "If you know that, it's more than I knew until a few minutes ago."

Her lips curled. The blue eyes chilled, and contempt was in her voice. "Why bother to pretend? We both know that Marie Hoe sent for you because you're a trained gun fighter, because she wants to get the men who arranged your brother's murder."

He was really startled. Grandmère had showed little interest in Marc's murderers. Why should this girl act as if she resented his coming because she feared that he might kill those murderers? It made no sense unless she were involved, or unless her family were involved. It was a new thought. In all the years that Grandmère had trailed Clayborne, hounding him with sly stories which ruined his chances and reputation in each new town he tried, the Claybornes had never once struck back.

Could things have changed here in Two Mile? Had Nell's father and brothers hired Marc's killer? Did this explain her poorly masked fear? He thought with bitterness that this offered still another check, another obstacle which would further prevent any friendship

15

with her. There was nothing he could say, nothing which might make her believe that he personally bore her family no ill will.

"I'd better go," he said, and turned back toward the street.

She was wordless, but after he passed the door he turned to find she was still watching him.

CHAPTER 3

THE ROCK MOUNTAIN BANK WAS A SINGLE-STORY building of native stone, looking like a vault with its narrow windows and dim, hushed interior. There was a high counter before three tellers' windows, a big safe against the rear wall, and three private offices which were reached by a gate through the counter.

Lester Hoe stopped at the first window where a small man, whose bald head glistened even in the dimness, examined him through the square panes of steel-rimmed spectacles.

"Are either Clint or Raoul here?"

The small man continued to peer, but before he answered the center-office door opened and Raoul appeared. He was a big man, almost two years older than Les, and in the time since they had met he had matured and put on weight. But despite the curling brown mustache and heavy sideburns framing his thickish face, he looked much the same.

"Raoul."

His brother nodded stiffly and came forward to open the gate, leading him back into the center office. Clint Hoe was at the roll-top desk. Of all the brothers, Clint alone had none of the Hoe darkness or Indian look. He

16

was a sandy-colored man, his hair already beginning to thin, his nose pointed, his blue eyes squinting a little, inclined to shift away under a steady gaze. He grunted when he saw Les, but the thin face held no more warmth than had Raoul's thick one.

Les surveyed them without feeling. As a child Raoul had bullied him and Clint had shrewdly forced him to do most of Clint's chores. In fact, he thought, even including Grandmère, there had never been much trust or love in the family relationships. Perhaps this had stemmed directly from the woman's unnatural coldness.

"A warm greeting." His tone was mocking. He crossed the room unasked and took a chair beside the window, tilting it and shoving his hat well back on his dark head.

"What made you expect a warm greeting?" Raoul made no effort to mask his resentment. "Clint and I stayed with Grandmère and Marc. We helped get established in this camp. We helped organize the mines and start the mill and the bank and the hotel, and now you show up with nothing behind you but the record of a hired gunman and try to take over."

Clint Hoe threw a look of annoyance at Raoul. It was not that he did not share his brother's resentment, but he was too devious a person to ever happily bring anything completely into the open. And he feared Les Hoe. He feared him, not because of the gun he wore, but because Les might find out things which would pull his carefully built house of cards to pieces.

He said, in a tone which he tried to make friendly but merely succeeded in making sound a little oily, "What Raoul is trying to say is that we don't resent you having your full just share of what the family has amassed, but we do feel that it's wrong for you to assume Marc's

17

place. Both of us had far more training, and things would be much better left in our hands."

Les Hoe could not quarrel with the idea behind the words. Certainly either one of them should know far more about running the business than he did. Had he trusted Clint more, he would have taken the statement at face value, but he knew, as only a younger brother can know, Clint's and Raoul's weaknesses, their petty concerns for their own interests, their absolute selfishness. Also, although he did not warmly love her, he had a high regard for Grandmére's judgement on everything except where Asa Clayborne was concerned, and he knew that her turning to him had been motivated by a deeper reason than simple family affection. For some reason of her own she did not relish committing her empire to Clint's or Raoul's management.

But he was too shrewd a poker player to expose his hand before the draw, before he learned about a number of things that at the moment puzzled him. He said coldly, "I didn't know what Grandmère had in mind. She said nothing in her letter except that it was imperative that I come."

Clint's lids dropped to mask his greedy eyes, and he sat perfectly still. Raoul shifted restlessly.

"I'm not sure I want to step into Marc's shoes."

"Then why did you come?" Raoul had never had the sense to keep his mouth shut.

Why had he come? Curiosity had played a major part in the decision—not to see the town, not to see his brothers or his grandmother or to find out how much they were worth. Not even to avenge Marc, for Marc was as much a stranger as these two, and his years as marshal had taught him the emptiness of vengeance. What then? Curiosity to know what had happened to

18

Nell Clayborne? It was amazing how the memory of her had lingered in his mind. He realized, of course, that his coming was probably too late, that it had probably always been to late for them; but there was no question that some potent force had drawn them together, ever since they had been children.

He ignored Raoul's question. "How did Marc die?" He did not care. It was a phrase, an effort to escape his own troubling thoughts.

They stared, not following his mind, and he knew that they were strangers, concerned only with their own welfare, that they would always be strangers as far as he was concerned. It was Clint who answered finally, after an interval as if he had weighed the words.

"Shot in the back. By the Claybornes, damn them."

Suddenly he recalled Nell Clayborne's manner, and his voice was tense when he said, "Which one?"

"Oh, they didn't do it themselves." Clint's voice was easy, as if he were on solider ground. "They hired it done, and the man who pulled the trigger died under the marshal's bullets, but they hired it done. If you don't believe me, ask Sarah Baker. She can tell the truth if she will."

Les Hoe started. "Sarah Baker? Is she in Two Mile?"

They watched him. Clint sounded slightly disconcerted. "You know her?"

He knew her, but he said merely, "She had a place in Deadwood. I wondered where she'd gone."

Raoul said viciously, "She's here all right, the bitch. Why Grandmère rents her the hotel bar is more than I know. It was in her place that Marc died. She lured him to his death, and then she laughed about it afterward."

Les Hoe straightened slowly. "Maybe I'll talk to her."

Raoul said, "It will do you no good. She is like a

19

hunk of ice. She has no nerves, no feelings of any kind. Money is the only thing she understands, and you haven't got enough."

Clint spoke wickedly from the desk. "He means he got no place with her and neither did Marc. All the girl said was 'Wait until your grandmother dies and you have the money. Then I'll talk to you.' That's why Marc slapped her. That's why she helped them kill him."

Les started for the door. Clint said nervously, "What are you going to do?"

He said honestly, "I don't know. I'll have to talk to Grandmère again." He went out, knowing that the men behind him were worried, and he thought, let them worry, it will do them good.

The hotel barroom had a street entrance as well as a wide doorway giving into the lobby. It was a big room, running the full depth of the building, its furnishings matching the lobby in richness. The bar and back bar were mahogany, and it was said that no finer existed either in Denver or San Francisco. Facing the bar, running along the side wall were gaming tables, poker, two faro layouts, and three roulette wheels. It was not yet noon, but the room was better than half-filled, both faro layouts running, one wheel, and games at four poker tables.

Les Hoe had spent many hours in gambling rooms. His work, both for Wells Fargo and as marshal of Deadwood, had necessitated his presence. Also, he was a natural gambler, but he had never seen such an orderly crowd except in Sarah Baker's Deadwood place.

He stopped just inside the door. From a long-ingrained habit he studied the people before him, searching for possible danger. Then he saw her, dealing at the center faro bank and moved forward. Once you

20

saw Sarah Baker you never forgot her. A slight girl, her age, Hoe guessed, was not over twenty-five. Her hair was a warm, coppery red, her eyes chocolate, soft and appealing. Yet there was nothing soft about her.

She had first run a gambling saloon in Denver, moving later to Deadwood, and he had known her for over three years in the Dakota town when, without warning or a word to him, she had sold the place and disappeared. He had not heard of her for a year and had no idea that she was in Two Mile.

That she could have had a hand in Marc's death he did not believe. During her time in Deadwood there had been no trouble in her place, and although every eligible male in the camp had made his advances, she had fended them off adroitly.

He moved forward to stand behind the players ringed at the layout and stood watching her. The classic face might have been carved from stone for all its change of expression as she drew the cards from the shoe.

The bets made, she glanced up, drawn by the pull of his eyes, and saw him. Her expression still did not alter, but after the play she signaled one of the floor men to take her place, and walked to the door beyond the head of the bar without again glancing at Hoe.

He held his place a full five minutes, then followed, pausing to knock gently on the panel.

"Come in, Les." The voice was low, throaty, with a warm huskiness. He pushed open the door.

She stood beside the window overlooking the rear alley which ran between the hotel and the canyon wall, and the sun, reflected from the rock, touched the highlights of her copper hair.

She said quietly, "I heard you were here," and stepped forward to give him her hand, her clasp firm

21

and impartial as a man's.

"I had no idea you were in Two Mile."

"Why should you?" She motioned to a chair. "And I had no idea the dashing marshal of Deadwood was a grandson of the Queen. I didn't associate the name until Marc was dead and I heard rumors you were on the way to avenge him."

"The rumors are wrong. I've been an officer long enough to let the law take its course." He sat down, and she took the chair behind the desk. "I came because Grandmère sent for me, and if the Claybornes are involved, I doubt that she'll want the murder avenged."

She lifted an eyebrow inquiringly. "Somehow those words don't make much sense, and yet, I've never before heard you say anything that didn't."

He watched her. Sitting in this office he experienced a relaxation he seldom knew. It had been the same in Deadwood. Her office was a sanctuary, and she had been the closest friend he had allowed himself in Dakota. Time and again her small warnings had helped, and twice they had saved his life. In return he had treated her as he would a man, respecting her obvious distaste for the romantic notions of many of her customers.

"It makes sense," he told her, "if you know something of Hoe history. The Queen, as you call her, is a Cajun from the Louisiana swamps, and those people know how to hate. Why she came upriver to Missouri is something she never told me, nor do I know why she hates Asa Clayborne as no man has ever been hated since the beginning of time. But ever since I was very small she has dedicated her life to trailing him, goading him, driving him from one camp to another. She would not want me, or anyone else, to kill him, because by dying he would escape her studied persecution."

"And you think the Claybornes had a hand in the murder?"

"My brothers say they did. They also tell me that you set it up."

She took no offense. She knew him well enough to know that he did not accept their suspicions. She said with her usual candor, "I did not like Marc. You know how I am with men, and he thought because I lease this place from your grandmother he had certain privileges. I told him no and he slapped me." Her slim hand with three tiny freckles across its back came up to touch her cheek. "He warned me what he would do, and I told him to wait until the Queen died, to wait until he was in her place, and he misunderstood. He thought that if he had the money I'd marry him. What I meant was that when the Queen died, when he was boss, I would move on."

Les did not speak.

"Raoul made the same mistake after Marc's death. How is it that you can be so decent and have such fools for brothers?"

He grinned, and the devil was back in his black eyes. "A lot of people don't think me decent, Sarah. To them I'm a hired killer."

"A lot of people don't consider me decent either." She matched his smile. "A woman running a saloon, a gambling hell. I must be as loose and depraved as they come."

He knew this was not true. In the camps gambling was as respectable as banking, and often more honestly operated, but few would understand how a good woman could manage such a business.

He said, "Apparently Grandmère trusts you. If she didn't, you would have been on your way."

23

"That's right."

"And would you say the Claybornes had something to do with Marc's murder?"

She took time to answer. "I don't know. Marc accused Sam Clayborne of being the head of high-graders and threatened to stop him. They were both in here, and Sam didn't even deny it."

He cocked an eyebrow. "High-graders?"

She nodded. "It's an open secret. The miners even joke about it. They steal more gold than they mine for the company, and they have to do something with what they steal. Figure it out for yourself. The Claybornes own the only mine not controlled by your grandmother. I've never been underground, but from report the Clayborne vein is small and badly fractured, yet their mill ships an amazing amount of gold each month."

He said, "I'm no miner. Can you explain more clearly?"

She shrugged. "I'm no miner either, but supposing miners stole high-grade ore from your grandmother's property. Supposing they sold it to one of the assay offices, which in turn sold it to the mill controlled by the Claybornes?"

He thought this over carefully. There had always been high-grading in all gold mines—the theft of rich, gold-bearing ore. In California, for instance, where the ore was free-milling, the theft had been simple. All the miner needed to do was to break the gold loose from the quartz matrix.

But in most Colorado districts the ores, were tellurides, complex, difficult and expensive to smelt, and without help the miner thief would be helpless to recover the gold from his stolen ore.

But if some mill owner like the Claybornes, with a

24

mill of their own, were willing to buy stolen high-grade, mix it with the product of their own mine, and mill it as if all the ore had come from their property, it would be nearly impossible to catch them, since their mine was also in Rock Mountain and the ore was probably nearly the same type as came from his grandmother's holdings.

"Are they getting rich?"

She said, "They seem to be doing all right. Up until last year I understand they were having a very rough time, then when high-grading increased, so did their ore shipments."

He wondered why Grandmère had not told him this, why Clint or Raoul had not explained the situation fully. Then his mind came back to the Claybornes and he asked, "If they are making so much money, why is Nell running the millinery shop?"

She gave him a slow glance, and there was a subtle change in her voice which he did not notice. "You know her?"

His laugh was a trifle self-conscious. "I was in love with her when we were both in the third grade."

Her gaze dropped, and her eyes apparently studied her desk, then she looked up and said slowly, considering, "I don't know your Nell. She has little use for me, like most of the women here, but I can guess that if she realizes what her family is doing, and she must since it is an open secret, she would not want to live on stolen money."

He nodded quickly, and she saw relief in his eyes and thought, he's still in love with her, and knew a kind of inner despair, for Sarah Baker was a realist who never tried to conceal facts from herself. She had had her problem and met it without flinching, building a protective wall between herself and the rest of the

25

world. When her growing friendship for Hoe had threatened to breach this wall, she had abruptly sold the Deadwood place and returned to Colorado, without telling him where she was going.

It was irony, she thought, that she had chosen Two Mile, where his family ran the town, but during the years she had known him Hoe had never mentioned any family, and she had concluded that the chance of relationship between him and the Queen was slight.

Now he was here, and she knew that her interest in him was a live and burning thing. She had thought that never again would any man stir her as Phil Baker had once done, but the knowledge that Les's interest was in Nell Clayborne and not in her cut like a knife, and it was with real relief that she heard the knock on the door and called, "Come in."

One of her floor men stepped in. She twisted in her chair to face him. "What is it, Harner?"

The man had the slim, expressionless face of the trained gambler, but now he seemed flustered, nervous, which was not natural.

"Talk to you a minute, Miss Sarah? It's important. Alone." He glanced toward Hoe.

Les Hoe rose at once. "I'll move along. It's been nice to see you, Sarah. I'll drop back later."

She watched him walk toward the door with a sense of reprieve, needing a chance to think, to reassess her own position before she talked to him again.

Hoe was thinking of Nell rather than of this girl as he came back into the gambling room. In the few minutes since he had left, the crowd had swelled. Men were now lined up two deep along the bar, and a second wheel was running. He hesitated, undecided about his next move, then turned toward the arch which connected the hotel lobby with the saloon. He would talk to Grandmère again, and he had about decided. He would not take her offer. There were many reasons for this, but primarily he had no desire to fight the Claybornes.

He moved through the crowd, at times having to sidestep to avoid being bumped, and thought nothing of it when a big man turned from the polished counter and blocked his path. The man had a wide, broad, animal face with a fleshy broken nose and thickened ear.

One glance showed Hoe that the man was or had been a professional fighter. Hoe stopped, side-stepped, and the big man moved with him, like a dancer following a partner.

Hoe stopped again. Until the man shifted he had thought this mere accident. Now his eyes narrowed. It wasn't. He stood flat-footed, ready. "Get out of my way." His tone was low, controlled.

The big man opened his mouth, exposing two broken teeth. "Who you ordering around, sport?"

Les Hoe moved a step backward and took an instant to glance around. Three men had shifted forward until he was boxed in a rough square. The rest of the crowd, always alive to the danger of trouble, had fallen back so that there was a clear space around them.

It was a trap. Hoe had no way of knowing who had set it or why, but it was a trap and he the victim. His brother Marc had died in this self-same room, only six weeks before, perhaps on this spot, perhaps cornered by these same men.

Who had ordered his death? He had never seen any of these men before. They were hired killers, killing without anger, without personal feeling, merely in the hope of gain.

Unless you are nearly an animal you never quite lose

the feeling of fear, no matter how many times you are called upon to face violence, and Les Hoe was afraid. But it was a studied fear, without panic, a fear which made him measure the odds and choose the course of action which offered him the best chance to survive.

Had he faced only the big fighter he would have drawn his gun and buffaloed him with the heavy barrel, depending on his known speed to strike before the other could free the gun tucked into the front of his belt over the bulging stomach.

But the moment he reached for his weapon the men behind him would draw, firing at him from four different directions. No man living would stand a chance in a spot like that.

He made no effort to draw, but his quick mind had already plotted his course of action. He took a slow step forward, measured, then another, making no hostile sign, no rapid gesture which would trigger them into crashing action.

They had not expected this. They were keyed for a sudden draw on his part, and they hesitated the barest instant, puzzled by his unwarlike manner, and in that instant he was almost touching the big fighter.

The man's reflexes were slow, but he came to with a start and threw a roundhouse crushing blow at the side of Hoe's head.

Hoe side-stepped at the last possible moment and, as the force of his own blow swung the big man half around, off balance, Hoe drove a short right viciously into the bulge of the stomach, just beside where the heavy gun nestled under the belt.

Breath driven from the fighter whistled through his loose lips. He bent double, paralyzed for the moment with pain, and might have fallen had not Hoe caught the back of his dirty collar, forced him erect, twisting him and locking his left arm under the bearded chin.

He stood thus, holding his victim as a huge shield, his back now to the lobby arch, facing the three who only a second before had him flanked.

Two already had their guns in hand, the third was just drawing. Hoe's right hand flashed down, lifting his heavy Colt from its holster in one continuous motion which swung up the long barrel to peer at them wickedly along the fighter's side.

He laughed suddenly, partly from relief, partly at the expressions of startled consternation which made them look like triplets, but mostly because violence always roused the devil that lurked within him, the devil of recklessness.

"Come and get me," he told them, and the laughter filled the silence of the room. "Come and get me, any time you've got the guts."

CHAPTER 4

ALL ACTION IN THE BIG ROOM WAS FROZEN, EVERY EYE centered on Hoe. No one tried to move. The crowd of miners, gamblers, businessmen stood as though their slightest gesture would trigger a volley of gunfire.

The three facing Hoe did not know quite what to do. In a single instant the play had been taken out of their hands and transferred to his.

The big fighter groaned and began to struggle. Hoe's voice, close to his ear, had a deadly quality which stilled him instantly. "Keep quiet or I'll blow you in two."

And then someone else took a hand in the game. Sarah Baker appeared in the doorway of her office, a

29

shotgun in her steady hands, a shotgun with its barrels sawed short.

"You. Drop those guns."

The gunmen facing Hoe had her at their backs. They hesitated for a moment, then reluctantly let the guns slide from their fingers.

"All right. Someone get Pierpont."

A floor man disappeared through the outer door. The rest of the crowd remained motionless. The minutes they waited seemed to stretch into hours. Actually, it was less than five minutes until the floor man was back, trailed by two men who wore small bronze stars pinned to their shirts.

Boyce Pierpont was as tall as Hoe and as dark. He wasted no time herding his prisoners ahead of him out to the street. The crowd in the room broke up. The games resumed, and Sarah Baker motioned Hoe to follow her into the office. Then she sent for the floor man who had interrupted their earlier conversation.

He arrived, glancing nervously from her to the silent Hoe.

"Shut the door." She was again at her desk the shotgun laid across its top.

"All right. Who sent you in here to get Hoe outside?"

His lips formed a denial. She cut it short. "Don't lie to me. I know you and the men you run with. Who was it?"

His voice was whining. "Honest, Sarah, I don't know what you're talking about."

Her eyes were hard, her mouth unrelenting. "Pick up your wages at the cashier. You're through."

Again the protest, and again she cut it short. "And tell your friends to keep out of my place. They killed one man in here. Next time I'll do the killing."

The man left hurriedly. Hoe said softly, "You certain

30

he had something to do with it?"

She nodded, her eyes still on the door.

"Who were the men who jumped me?"

"The bruiser is Carl Henney. He fought in the California camps and now he calls himself the Champion of Colorado. The others don't count."

"Who are they working for?"

She considered. "The easy thing would be to say the Claybornes, but I don't know. Henney has at times worked for your brothers. He even worked here as a bouncer, and has done odd jobs for your grandmother."

"What will happen to them?"

She shrugged. "Nothing. Pierpont will keep them in jail overnight. They'll be fined ten dollars apiece for wearing guns in the town limits, and turned loose. If I hadn't sent for Pierpont even that much wouldn't be done. There's an anti-gun ordinance here, but it's seldom enforced."

He said, "I haven't thanked you for taking a hand. You made some enemies this morning."

Her shrug was more expressive than words. "Les, are you going to work for your grandmother?"

"I haven't decided." He roamed around the room like a restless cat, pausing to stare out of the window.

"Then why do you stay? The next time they move after you they'll pick a better spot."

He turned around. His smile was almost gentle. "I'm used to it," he said. "Wherever I go someone feels they have to take a shot at me. Unless I run off somewhere and change my name I suppose I'll always be Les Hoe, marshal of Deadwood, and every gun-crazy kid who wants to build himself a reputation will figure I'm a fair target."

She knew exactly what he meant. He was marked, as

31

she was marked. Sarah Baker, gambler. At the thought her mouth thinned down and there was bitterness in her eyes. She knew that to many people her position and occupation had glamour and drew envy. To herself it was a case of necessity, a way of meeting obligations which she did not want to avoid.

"I should have kept quiet," she said. "I have no right to offer you advice."

"You have every right. I would guess that you are the only friend I have in Two Mile." He came toward her and did something he had never done before, bending and kissing her forehead gently.

"Thanks again for helping, and don't worry about me. A lot of men have found me difficult to kill."

She sat quiet long after he had left the office, her eyes on the window without seeing it. His friend. The words brought back her bitterness. Friend. She did not want him as a friend. But he would never be anything else. Of this she was certain, even if she had been free to have it otherwise. There was Nell Clayborne. She knew clearly that it was the presence of the Clayborne girl which would hold him in Two Mile. She had read that in his eyes.

Les Hoe was also thinking about Nell Clayborne as he crossed the hotel lobby and mounted the stairs to knock on the door of his grandmother's rooms.

He had made up his mind to force a showdown with Grandmère, to make the old woman lay her full cards on the table. He heard his grandmother's voice in response to his knock, and went in to find her before a paper-littered desk near the window. She did not look up as he entered and took a chair beside the desk. She went on writing.

"So, you managed to get yourself into trouble already."

His surprise showed. She raised her head, putting down her pen, and said, "You needn't look thunderstruck. Nothing goes on in this hotel that is not reported to me at once, and very little that goes on in the town."

"Then probably you can tell me who ordered this attack."

"I can't, but Henney can."

"If he would."

"He will." Her voice was grim. "I've already sent for him."

As if in answer, there came a knock at the door. She called and the door opened to expose the ex-fighter, Boyce Pierpont behind him.

The fighter stood uncertainly in the opening, but Pierpont made up his mind for him by planting a flat hand in the man's back and pushing. Henney took three stumbling steps forward before he regained his balance.

"Take off your hat." It was the marshal.

The fighter glared at him like a cornered animal, but he cuffed off the broken headgear.

Grandmère said, "You've got no sense, Carl. No sense at all."

The man's tongue came out to run around bruised lips, but he did not answer.

"You think you can fight me and still stay in Two Mile?"

Henney shrugged, sullen.

"Who set you up to this, and what did they pay you?"

Pierpont said in his flat voice, "He had a hundred dollars in his pocket."

Henney glared at the marshal again, hate in his

33

lowering eyes.

"Who paid you?"

"No one. He got in my way." For the first time since entering the room Carl Henney looked directly at Les Hoe.

"And you just happened to have three friends with guns to back you up." The woman rose. She looked very small standing beside the big desk. "Hand me that whip, Les."

Hoe had not noticed the whip, coiled on the table behind him. It had a three-foot handle and ten feet of buckskin lash, split at the end, and each tail beaded with metal. He did not need to be told that those tails could cut a man's back or face to ribbons.

He said easily, not moving, "I don't need a woman to fight my battles, Grandmère."

Temper flared in her prominent eyes. "This is my town, boy, and I run it the way I want. Hand me the whip."

"Get it yourself." He took a perverse delight in angering her.

She stood a moment longer, then flung about and crossed to the table and picked up the whip. With a flick of her surprisingly strong wrist she snapped out the long lash to run across the floor like an uncoiling snake.

Henney's heavy cheeks had whitened under the grubby patches of his days-old beard. "You ain't going to let her whip me?" He was appealing to the marshal.

Pierpont laughed, a dry, hacking sound without humor. "I don't know how to stop her."

The whiplash whistled suddenly as she brought it back and then over her head. The tails licked out, wrapping their loaded ends around his thick, dirty neck.

He cried out like a child, trying to catch the biting

34

leather before she could retrieve it. But her wrist was too quick and she swept the lashes out of his grasp. He folded his arms about his face then, elbows out, and crouched almost double to offer as little target as possible, moaning as he dropped to his knees.

Les Hoe had a momentary desire to laugh. The picture was comical, this huge toad of a man who could have broken Grandmère in one hand groveling there, burying his head like an ostrich.

"Don't, don't!" It was Henney, pleading from the shelter of his heavy arms.

The lash whistled again, this time striking the curved back, cutting the shirt like a sharp knife, bringing a splatter of blood as it crisscrossed the skin.

"You ready to talk?"

There was a blubbering response.

"Who paid you?"

"Sam Clayborne."

"All right. Get out, and if I see you in this town again I'll aim for your eyes next time. Turn him loose, Pierpont."

The marshal nodded. He put a hand under the fighter's armpit and hoisted him toward the door. When they had gone Marie Hoe and her youngest grandson looked at each other.

She coiled the whip and replaced it on the table. "And you think you're tough."

He smiled. "It was a wonderful performance."

She went around the desk and glared at him. "You think I was acting?"

"I think it's an easy thing to beat a man when you have a marshal standing behind him. You're a fraud, Grandmère. You trade on being a woman. No man would ever beat another when there was a gun holding

35

him still."

She, sniffed. "You've got mighty nice ideas for a hired killer."

He let that pass.

"Are you going to shoot Sam Clayborne?"

He watched her. "Do you want me to? I thought you wanted the Claybornes to live. If they died you could no longer pester them."

Her lids dropped to mask her eyes. "I don't want Asa killed. What happens to his children is no affair of mine."

He eased himself against the edge of the table. "Grandmère, I never asked you before. Why do you hate Clayborne so much?"

Her fingers tightened until her hands became small fists. "Never mind. It has nothing to do with you."

He said seriously, "I don't care what happens to the Judge, or to his boys. They should be able to look after themselves. I saw Nell in the hat shop. I won't sit quiet and see her hurt."

She made no effort to conceal her anger. "You think you're still in love with her. You always did act like a sick puppy when she was around."

He did not deny it.

"Look." Her tone had changed. "I care nothing about the girl, but for your own good keep away from her."

Still he did not answer, and she changed the subject. "Are you going to move in and take Marc's place?"

"I don't know yet."

"You're going to have to decide, and soon. There are things which have to be done, now."

"I'll tell you later, tonight." He straightened and moved toward the door. Afterward, sitting alone in her fancy room, Marie Hoe did something which she had seldom done in her life. She bent her head and cried, whispering as she did so, "Les, you don't have the guts. You aren't a Hoe. I don't ever want to hear of you again."

CHAPTER 5

NELL CLAYBORNE WAS JUST ABOUT TO CLOSE THE SHOP when the outer door opened and the small warning bell tinkled. She spent a moment straightening the work table before she brushed aside the curtain between herself and the front of the shop. Then she stopped, still holding the curtain. Les Hoe faced her across the counter.

Her first strong emotion was surprise. Her next was a rush of pointless anger, not at him, that he had dared to come back, but at herself, for she suddenly knew that deep inside she was glad to see him.

Nell Clayborne's life had not been a happy one. When she was a child her father had been a leading lawyer at the Cape, and his family had held the top position in local society. But since their first move West their fortunes had gone steadily downhill, and she had found few friends or associates in the cattle towns and the mining camps through which her father's restless feet had led them.

It had been worse here in Two Mile than in any other town. For one thing, Marie Hoe, whom her father hated, had prospered here while the Clayborne fortunes had declined rapidly. Then, too, the actions of her father and her two brothers distressed her. She was unhappily aware that they were buying stolen ore through their assay offices, running it with the ore from their mine through the mill.

Even before her discovery of their practice she had entertained the idea of a millinery shop. She was handy with a needle, for years had made her own hats, but her father violently opposed her working, and her brothers had sided with him.

The opening of the shop had led to a rift. She had moved to the Peck boarding house on the other side of the canyon and seldom saw her family now.

To her mind Les Hoe represented the period of her life which had been carefree and happy. That she had never been allowed to play with him during the school years had only heightened her curiosity about him, and this curiosity was tugging at her now as she stepped forward, letting the curtain fall behind her.

"Did you want something?" Her tone was still unfriendly but not as acid as it had been that morning.

His quick smile lighted his dark eyes, and his voice was a trifle mocking. "I don't suppose you'd believe me if I said I'd come to buy a hat?"

She said steadily, "I wouldn't be surprised. I heard you were more than friendly with that gambler woman."

He sobered at once. "Where did you hear that?"

"There is very little gossip in a town of this size that is not discussed in a dress or hat store, and your arrival created more comment than anything that has happened in a long while. I know you were sitting in Sarah Baker's office before Henney led the attack on you. I know that you and she are apparently old friends."

He nodded. "There would be no point in denying it even if I wished to, and I don't. Sarah Baker is as fine a woman as I have ever known."

"I judge that in your profession you know a great many of the wrong kind."

Suddenly he was angry with her. Suddenly he wanted to reach across the low counter, grasp her slender shoulders in his big hands, and shake her thoroughly. He didn't, but he did say in a voice sharpened by his anger, "Don't judge people, Nell, especially on appearances. You would usually be wrong. That is one thing a marshal does learn. Those who seem the best are sometimes the worst."

She said coolly, "I am not intending to judge Sarah Baker or anyone else. If she prefers to run a gambling house and associate only with men, that is her business. I do not even try to judge your grandmother or your brothers."

He changed the subject abruptly. "I came here to offer a truce to your family. I want to talk to Sam and Lloyd and your father."

"Why?"

He could not tell her that his resolve was prompted by solicitude for her. He could not tell her that he had loved her ever since the third grade. He knew the whole thought was utterly foolish. They actually were two strangers whose lives had run in different patterns.

He said instead, "Perhaps I feel that I owe something for what my family has done to yours through the years. Perhaps I'm tired of trouble. Perhaps I don't like having men box me in an effort to kill me."

She said sharply, "Are you saying that my brothers hired Henney and his crew?"

"I didn't say it, Henney did."

"I don't believe you."

"I'm not surprised you don't. Still, I'm not lying."

His tone seemed to convince her. "If Henney did say that, I'm surprised you haven't gone after them already. That is what I'd expect from what I know of you."

"How much do you actually know about me?"

She started to call him a man who made his living by the gun. Then she stopped, realizing that actually all she did know was only hearsay, and she was too honest a person not to admit it. "Maybe I'm wrong. Maybe you're not as bad as I supposed."

It was the first break in her defenses, and he knew a rush of encouragement. "Nell, why should we fight? We've known each other a long time. I used to think I was in love with you when we were kids."

Sudden color came up to stain her cheeks. She hesitated a long moment, then said in a low voice, "There is something I've remembered all these years, something I'm sorry for. You asked me to a party once, and I said I couldn't come because you were river trash."

"Forget it."

"It was one of those things you can't forget. It rises out of my memory at night when I can't sleep, and makes me writhe. All this time I have wanted the chance to say that I'm sorry." She was very intent, her eyes pleading with him to believe, and suddenly he knew that he could have kissed her. He knew it by instinct, but he repressed the rising desire. The time was not yet.

Instead he said, "Forget it. It's something I've forgotten long ago." He lied, but he would do more than lie to comfort her. "Listen, Nell, my grandmother did not bring me back here to find Marc's murderer. She brought me back to take Marc's place, to take over the management of the Hoe interests."

She was watching him, not quite understanding.

"I have no fight with your family. I know that they've been hounded from one camp to the next, driven by lies half truths which were whispered about them by my

40

grandmother and my brothers, but believe me, I never had any part in that."

She still found no words, and he went on. "I haven't made up my mind as yet whether to take her offer or not. If I do, it will have to be on my own terms. I refuse to play the part Marc played, to let Grandmère do my thinking for me. And I refuse to carry on this senseless feud with you Claybornes."

She wet her lips. "You're trying to say something that isn't possible. That horrible old woman will never leave my father alone until he dies."

"We'll see." Hoe's voice was grim. "But first, before I decide, I want to talk to your father."

She showed her surprise. "Talk to him—what about?"

He said sternly, "About high-grading," and watched the expression of her face change, and hurried to explain. "I'm going to offer them a deal. If they will stop buying high-grade ore at their mill, I will undertake to make Grandmère stop her persecutions. Is that fair?"

Suddenly she was smiling. Suddenly without seeming to realize what she did she leaned across the counter and squeezed his arm. "If you only could, if you would make them stop so I could sleep again, I could face people on the street."

He sensed suddenly what the knowledge of her family's acts had meant to her, and his feeling of protectiveness increased. "Stop worrying," he said. "Between us well bury the Clayborne-Hoe feud. Now, will you tell your father I want to see him?"

"I'll do better than that. I'll take you up to the house. I'll make them talk to you. I'll make them listen. Wait." She turned back to the workroom and got a light shawl, which she pulled around her shoulders.

As they moved up First Street in the half light of the

41

late summer evening she was very conscious of the curious stares from the people they met, and she knew that the story that Nell Clayborne had been walking with a Hoe would be all over town in minutes. The feud was an open thing, dividing the town into two factions. Hoe also noted the interest their progress made, but ignored it. He was used to being stared at, used to being the center of attention.

Like most houses in Two Mile the Clayborne place sat well above street level, reached by steep steps, clinging to the canyon wall, for there was very little level ground in the whole townsite.

The hall smelled unaired, carrying faint odors of old food and stale tobacco smoke, and there was no lamp, the only light a yellow glare from the open doorway at the rear.

Nell called out as they entered the house, and the sound of voices which had made a kind of undertone in the rear room died.

"Who is it?" Les recognized the Judge's voice, although he had not heard it for years.

"Nell."

There was silence for a long moment, and in that instant she led Hoe forward to the room. Three men in shirt sleeves sat there, the table between them littered with assay slips and mill sheets. Asa Clayborne sat at the far side, facing the door. He was a handsome man, nearing seventy. His lion's head was proud, and his white hair was long, a mane. He had altered little since the days so long ago when his ringing voice had dominated the elections at the Cape, for Clayborne was a natural orator, a rabble rouser who supplemented his law practice with one political office after another.

Sam, sitting on his father's left, was some ten years older than Hoe, and, at thirty-six, a younger replica of the father. Lloyd, three years Sam's junior, resembled his mother's people, being slight, dark, almost womanish. At the moment the three shared a common emotion—surprise.

"Hoe." It was Asa. He turned hard eyes on his daughter. "What's the meaning of this?"

She said steadily, "He wants to talk to you, and I knew that unless I came along you would refuse to listen."

Clayborne's face had flushed, but it dulled slowly to an unhealthy gray, the only indication of his age. His blue eyes came back to measure the visitor and his goatee bobbed a little as he said, "Since you've forced your way in. here, talk."

His sons had not moved. Lloyd had no gun, but there was a belt around Sam's waist and his hand had dropped toward it unconsciously as he slowly stood up.

Hoe ignored him, saying to Asa, "Don't you think this feud foolishness has gone far enough, Judge?" The title stemmed from the days when Clayborne had served one term on the bench.

Asa Clayborne took himself very seriously, and his life very seriously, and his hate very seriously. He said now in full voice, "Did that miserable woman send you?"

Les Hoe had never heard Grandmère referred to as a miserable woman, and his lips quirked, but his voice was flat, even, as he answered. "No one sent me. I speak solely for myself. But I learned in Deadwood that few differences can't be settled if both sides are willing to talk things out."

The Judge's eyebrows bushed whitely and he stared

out beneath them, glowering as if Les were a criminal brought before the bar. "And just what prompted this unheard-of action."

"Maybe I'm a little ashamed of some of the things my family has done. I know how they've dogged you across this country for years."

Clayborne drew a long, tortured breath, trying to control his anger. When he spoke his voice was surprisingly mild. "They certainly have done that. Marie Hoe has come as near ruining my life as one person can ruin another's, but we may even the score yet."

"By buying stolen ore from high-graders?" He saw Sam Clayborne stiffen at the words, saw the man's fingers curl around his gun butt, and said sharply, "Don't lift it, Sam. I'd kill you before it was out of the leather."

Sam Clayborne froze. They watched each other a long moment. It was the Judge who broke the tension. "Let go the gun, Sam."

Slowly the tautness ran out of his big son. He released the gun and let his hand fall loosely at his side. "Whether you can kill me or not is not the question." His voice had the same booming quality that marked his father's. "I don't like to be called a thief."

"They tell me you laughed when Marc called you that before his death."

They watched him, saying nothing, and he turned his attention back to the Judge. "I'm offering a deal. If you want to deny buying high-grade, deny it, but the fact remains that Marc is dead and that four men tried to kill me this morning in the Baker place."

Asa said slowly, "Are you accusing us of having something to do with those attacks?"

"Henney says you paid him one hundred dollars to

brace me."

"He lies." The words broke from Sam Clayborne. "What reason would we have to want you killed? I haven't seen you since you were a brat."

"And Marc?"

The man's mouth opened in protest, but his father silenced him. "I thought you said you'd come here to end the feud."

"I have. When I came into town everyone expected me to go hunting Marc's murderer. I will. If I find out who killed him, I'll take the evidence to the marshal. I worked for the law too long to want to take things into my own hands. This has nothing to do with the feud. Henney says you tried to have me killed."

"I tell you he lies. I never had anything to do with Henney in my life. He has worked for your brothers and your grandmother, never for me. Are you sure he wasn't lying, maybe on orders, trying to blame us for something someone else ordered?"

"He was being whipped."

They turned to each other, then back to him. There was shock in Nell's face. "Whipped by you?"

"By Grandmère."

Sam Clayborne swore under his breath. "The old hag thinks she's God. If she were only a man! If you could fight her as you fight a man!"

Les said, "I'm a man. I'm taking over the Hoe interests, and I'm going to run them my way. I told you I'm tired of this senseless feud, that I'll end it if you stop high-grading. I'll see that you are no longer interfered with in any way. That's fair, isn't it?"

He read negation in their faces and his voice hardened. "Don't push me. I'm trying to be fair because I realize the wrongs piled up on your side. But I have no

45

intention of sitting quiet and allowing anyone to steal the company blind. Good night."

He turned then without waiting for an answer and stalked down the hall. He had reached the porch when he heard Nell running behind him and turned.

She was breathless. She grasped both his arms, not conscious of what she was doing. "Thank you," she said. "Thank you for understanding, for trying to help. I'll talk to them. I'll make them stop buying ore. I'll make them." Then as if fearing she had said too much, she turned and ran back into the house.

CHAPTER 6

LES HOE TALKED TO HIS GRANDMOTHER IN HER SUITE until after midnight, and he laid his cards on the table for her to see. "I'm not buying any of your fight with Clayborne," he told her. "Whatever grudge you think you have against Asa has been written off long ago. You've turned his life into a perfect hell. The man has presence and ability and charm. Without you dogging him at every step, telling lies, telling sly stories against his honesty, he might have gone far in politics. He might even have gone to the Senate."

She watched, her eyes silent, brooding.

"Instead he's a broken-down mining-camp lawyer, owning a small mill, a worthless mine, forced to buy high-grade to exist."

She flared at that. "No one ever forced Asa Clayborne to do anything. The man is a liar and a fool, and I'll strip him clean before I'm through."

He rose. "Not with my help you won't." He started for the door.

"Stop."

He stopped, but he did not turn. Behind him a struggle of some kind was going on within Grandmère's shrunken breast. When she spoke there was a choked sound in her voice and she had begun to cry.

He was too amazed to recall his anger. He turned, coming back to stand before her, watching the small body shudder with her racking sobs.

When she could control herself she said in a smothered voice, "Go ahead, make what terms you will, but take things over. Run them, run them like a man."

"Grandmère."

She said bitterly, "You would have had to know sooner or later, but I wanted your agreement first, and don't tell Clint or Raoul. Raoul would blab it all over town. Clint would try and turn things to his own advantage. The fact is that I'm broke."

"Broke?" The news shocked him as nothing else would have. It was not the loss of the money. He had never actually cared too much about money, but he was puzzled. "But the fifteen million shares of stock in the mine, the bank, the mill, this hotel?"

She said levelly, "Fifteen million shares can be a liability when things go wrong. Sit down, I'll try to explain."

He took a place on the sofa. "It's the high-grading," she began. "We don't know exactly, but the miners stole something between five and ten million last year."

Since his top salary had never been over two hundred dollars a month, the figures appalled him.

"The ore they leave," she went on, "the stuff they contemptuously call company ore, is so low grade that it barely pays the cost of milling. The mine hasn't earned a dollar for nearly a year, and last January we had a bad

47

cave-in at the Diamond Extension. It cost two hundred thousand to clear the tunnel, and it shut down a third of the mine. We didn't have enough in the treasury to do the work. We had to assess the stockholders half a million dollars to clean out the mine and get more working capital. My share was over three hundred thousand. I raised it by mortgaging this hotel and selling most of my bank stock."

He whistled softly. "So what do you expect me to do?"

She said quickly, "Stop the high-grading. If we could mill all the ore we mine we'd be out of trouble in sixty days. There's still a fortune left in Rock Mountain."

"But haven't you already tried?"

She nodded wearily. "We've had the company police arrest men as they come off shift, and we've found ore hidden on most of them, but the local courts count on the miner vote which Asa Clayborne organized during the last election. All they give them are small fines and a warning which means nothing."

"You did nothing else?"

"Marc tried to close the crooked assay offices. There are over a hundred in town, ninety-five of them buying stolen ore. It does no good. As soon as Pierpont closes one, two more are opened. The only way to stop it is to put in change rooms, or close the Clayborne mill, or both."

He had a picture of Asa Clayborne and his sons, at their table, poring over the mill reports. "They must be getting rich."

She said, "They're getting a good part, but don't forget, every miner who carries out ore under his shirt and every crooked assayer who acts as a middleman or fence is also cutting into the pie. The money is split a

48

thousand ways, perhaps more. There are over seven thousand men working underground."

He whistled again.

There was malice in her eyes as she asked, "Do you still think your friends the Claybornes will stop high-grading just because you ask them to?"

He had the sudden certainty that they would not. He did not know how much Asa Clayborne knew about Grandmère's finances, but certainly the man had cause for trying to drive Marie Hoe to the wall, and his mind turned to the other alternative.

"What about change rooms?" He had heard of the change rooms that had originated in California, rooms where the miners, coming off shift, were forced to change their clothes under the watchful eye of company police.

She said, "We decided on that six months ago. We announced what we were going to do, and at once the miners rebelled. But we were going ahead with it anyway. And then Marc was murdered, and I have made no further effort. I have been waiting for you."

He said warningly, "I have no training in business, Grandmère."

"That's your fault, not mine," she told him sharply.

"Perhaps Raoul or Clint would do better."

"You believe that?"

He did not believe it. What was coming shaped up as one of the biggest fights in history. He knew this by instinct, and he also knew that neither of his brothers had the stomach for a fight. He rose.

"Let me think about it tonight. Meet me at the bank at eleven in the morning. I'll tell you then what seems to me the best to try, and I'll also tell Raoul and Clint."

She let him go, her old mouth pulled down at the

corners her usually smooth face shrunken and lined. "He's the only hope I have," she thought desperately, "and he won't do. I guess you win after all, Asa. I guess I'm through."

In the hall outside her door Les Hoe paused, thinking. He had never felt so inadequate in his life. He knew he needed advice, expert advice, and he had no idea where to find it or whom to trust. And then he thought of Sarah Baker and went quickly down, crossed the lobby, and entered the gambling room.

His searching eyes failed to find the girl at any of the games, and he rounded the end of the bar to knock on her office door.

She was at her desk, busy with accounts, and she threw down her pen wearily as he came in.

"Am I interrupting?"

"I'm glad of an excuse to stop. Can I order you a drink?"

He shook his head and settled into a chair beside the desk, saying, "You work so hard. This is no life for a pretty woman."

"From another man I would suspect the opening. From you, I know that you have nothing in mind and I can relax." Her grin was friendly. She was striving to keep their relationship on the easy, impersonal footing it had had in Deadwood.

"Actually I've come for advice, but I'd like to talk about you first. You worry me. You have nothing at all, no outside friends, no time off, no pleasures. You say you can relax with me, but do you relax? In all the time I've known you, you have never once mentioned anything about yourself, your life before you started all this."

"Don't pry, Les."

"I'm not prying, but I always bring my troubles to you, and you never return the compliment."

"What is it now?"

"I've decided to take Marc's job. I've got to stop the high-grading. I've seen the Claybornes. I've tried to make a deal. I doubt if they'll take it."

"Because of the girl?"

He nodded slowly. "Partly, partly because the trouble of Grandmère's making."

"The girl. It's the girl you're worrying about, isn't it? You love her?"

"If you can love a person you hardly know." He searched for words. "I can't get her out of my mind. It's been that way always, and I've always known she was too good for me."

Sarah said earnestly, "No one's too good for you, Les. No one, believe me."

He was startled by the depth of feeling her voice betrayed. She realized it, and color flooded her cheeks. "I'm sorry, Les, I shouldn't have said that."

There was strain in her voice, strain in the room, a new awareness which Les had never experienced with her before.

"Sarah, I—"

She said brusquely, "Forget it. Once in a while I slip and forget that I'm no longer a woman. I never talk about myself and I'm not going to start now, but I will say this so you don't worry about me. I am not free. I'll probably never be free. That's why I have nothing to do with men even when they are as attractive as the former marshal of Deadwood. Now, what's the problem you want to talk about?"

He hesitated, then told her. "Grandmère broke down tonight and cried. I never saw her do that before."

51

"Cried?"

He repeated then, almost word for word, what the older woman had said, and she listened in intent silence. When he finished, she spoke slowly. "I knew about the stockholders' assessment. I even knew she had borrowed money but I had no idea her affairs were in that serious condition."

"These high-graders have apparently robbed the mine blind."

She nodded. "There never has been a town like this for money spent. I see common miners who get four dollars a day, here at my tables, making hundred-dollar bets. I see them in the finest restaurants, spending money like millionaires. It makes for wonderful general business, seven thousand miners with stolen money in their pockets. Do you wonder that a number of the merchants would be as sorry to see it stop as the miners would be?"

"It can't go on."

"How will you stop it?"

His jaw set, and she saw a glint in his eyes which she had seen only once or twice before. "If the Claybornes won't listen to reason and stop buying stolen ore at their mill, I'll put in change rooms. I'll stop it if I have to strip every miner comming off shift myself. Listen to me, Sarah. It isn't only the mining company. You say the merchants would hate to see it stop, that they would back the miners. Don't the fools realize that if the company goes broke, if the mines close, this town will fold overnight? You've seen camps fade, so have I, and when they do, everyone loses."

She said tensely, "I'm afraid you're fighting a losing battle. What you say is true, but it's hard to tell a man who's making four dollars a day for ten hours

52

underground that he should save that job by giving up a hundred a day in stolen ore. He would laugh at you, and many of the storekeepers would laugh. Maybe you can whip the Claybornes into shape, but you'll never put in change rooms. Seven thousand miners aren't going to let you."

"I'm going to try."

"Then you'd better talk to O'Shea."

"And who is O'Shea?"

"The head of the local union. He's honest, and if you can make him understand what you've been telling me, he might just try to help. The trouble is that your grandmother never recognized his organization and the membership is small. Men care little about basic wages when they can steal twenty times as much on any shift. It's even whispered that many of them actually pay the foreman to get their jobs."

"Why didn't you tell me all this when I first talked to you?"

Her brown eyes were very frank, and she pushed the bronze hair back from her high forehead with the back of a hand. "I know you. I knew that if you understood the problem, you'd stay, and I did not want you to stay. I don't want you killed."

His voice was low, his eyes probing. "Sarah, do I really mean a lot to you?"

She said rapidly, "Don't push, Les. There's nothing for you, nothing for me, but my world has been a better place because I knew you. Let's let it ride at that. Think that you have one friend, that anything I can do to help is at your service. If you need money, I have managed to save a little. What I have is yours."

"Sarah." He had risen.

"No, you'd better go. I haven't talked to a man this

53

way for nearly seven years, and I don't expect to again, ever."

"Sarah, I think you owe me something."

"What?"

"To tell me what you are talking about. You have a right to build a front against the world, but not against me."

She sat hunched so that he could see only the top of her red-brown head; then she looked up and there was a faint smile on her well-formed lips. "Never mind. I was feeling sorry for myself. It's something I seldom do."

"Why not tell me? You've held it alone a long time."

She sighed. "There's really not much to tell. I married a man named Phil Baker seven years ago, and within six months he developed tuberculosis. He had to come to a dry climate so I brought him to Denver. He's still there, in a bed at a sanitarium, and he'll never be up again. I had to support him. I had no training, but I noticed there were more saloons, more gambling rooms than anything else, so I opened one."

He did not speak, and she went on steadily. "I'm married, yet I'm not married. I have not lived with a man in seven years. Phil will never be up again, but he may breathe twenty years."

Les Hoe had always admired her, but never before felt sorry for her. A girl, young then, maybe not yet twenty, with a sick husband, in a strange raw frontier town, she had dared to take probably her last dollar and open a business with which she was utterly unfamiliar. He said, "I don't know how you did it. I don't know how you managed to succeed."

She smiled faintly. "If I had known as much then as I know now, I'd have lacked the courage to try, but sometimes fear makes you brave, and there was an old man at my boardinghouse who had run gambling rooms most of his life. He was broke and I had ten thousand dollars. Maybe a sensible person would have saved the money, living on it carefully until it was exhausted, but I've never been able to just sit and wait. We opened our place. My partner lived only a few months, but in that time he had taught me many things, given me the confidence I needed."

"There are few women who could have done it."

She said, "You might be surprised what women can do when they are driven by desperation, but I'll tell you one thing. The day after Phil dies my place, wherever I am then, will close. It will have served its purpose, and once that purpose is gone, I'm through."

He said, "Sarah, I—"

She rose. She stopped what he might have said by placing a firm hand across his lips. "No, get out. Leave me alone a little while to regret that I have talked too much."

He realized that she meant it. He pressed his lips against the palm which still covered his mouth, turned, and left the room without a word.

For some reason her story had shaken him more than had the news of his grandmother's trouble. He knew that he should get some sleep, but at the moment sleep was impossible. He threaded his way through the milling crowd and felt the welcome coolness of the thin air on his face. It was long past midnight, but the street still crawled with loaded wagons and the sidewalks were far from empty.

He turned up the main thoroughfare. He had no point of destination in mind. He only wanted to walk, to think. And his abstraction was so deep that he did not see the big man lurking in the alley mouth until he passed, until the heavy voice said, "Don't turn. I want to talk to you."

He had only heard the voice twice, but he knew instantly that it was Carl Henney, and his shoulders tensed in expectation. He wondered vaguely whether Henney meant to shoot him, or pound him into senselessness with those huge fists.

CHAPTER 7

HENNEY MOVED UP BEHIND HIM. HE COULD HEAR THE scuff of the fighter's big feet on the splintered sidewalk boards. In his days as marshal this could never have happened. Then he had never walked a block without examining if for potential danger.

His fleeting thought was that this man was a mark of the change which had been wrought in him during his short time in Two Mile. His preoccupation before coming here had been centered on danger, danger to himself, to the men who worked with him, and to the town.

But now his mind focused on larger, more abstract problems. Instinctively he glanced along the street for possible aid, but at the moment there were no pedestrians within a half block of them, and the teamsters of the passing wagons paid him no attention, concentrating fully on their teams.

Henney's breath was on his neck and he wondered why the man had not already pulled the trigger or swung his heavy weapon to bring the barrel crashing down across his skull.

Long training held him motionless. Movement might make a nervous man squeeze away a shot, and every moment the shot was delayed increased his chances of survival. And then Henney's gravel voice muttered, almost in his ear, "Don't touch your gun. All I want is to talk to you."

Les Hoe had the sudden bursting desire to break into foolish laughter. His nerves were taut, tighter than they had ever been in his whole life, and the reaction was like a tidal wave threatening to engulf him.

He steadied his voice with effort. "Talk, then."

Henney's voice was a little jumpy, as if his own nerves were none too steady. "I'm putting my gun away. You can turn now."

Les Hoe turned slowly. In the half darkness of the street he could see Henney's battered features only indistinctly. The man stood between him and the light coming from the hotel bar, his big body a silhouette, his face in shadow.

"What's this all about?"

Henney said, 'You didn't help whip me this morning. You wouldn't even hand her the whip."

"That's right."

"Damn her, and damn your family. I owe them nothing. but I've got nothing against you."

Hoe did not speak. He had questioned enough criminals to know that there is a certain moment when, goaded by anger or fear or revenge, almost any man will talk.

Henney licked his lips. It was obvious that he was having a hard time forcing out the words. "I was supposed to say that Sam Clayborne hired me to set you up. I was supposed to put the blame on the Judge and his family, but I wasn't paid to get whipped, and now your grandmaw has ordered me out of town and Pierpont would love nothing better than to put a bullet in my gut."

"Why don't you leave, then?"

"Pierpont took every cent I had. I asked for it back to leave, and he laughed. He told me to walk, and it's near twenty miles to Teal's place, and there's nothing in between."

Les Hoe said softly, "How much do you want?"

Henney spat. "I was given a hundred to kill you."

Les Hoe laughed in spite of himself. "You've got gall, he said. "You admit you were hired to kill me. Do you expect me to match the figure you were given?"

"I could have killed you a minute ago. I could have taken the money from your pocket, or gone back to the men who hired me in the first place. They would have paid again if you were dead."

"So I should pay you merely because you spared my life?"

"It should be worth a hundred for you to know who they are."

"All right. Tell me who they are. If I think the information is worth it, you get your hundred."

Henney rubbed the side of his thick nose thoughtfully. "I trust you. It was your brothers."

Les Hoe was not surprised. He had had more than a half-formed suspicion in his mind. Henney could be lying, of course. This might be a Clayborne ruse to split him from his brothers, but even in that case he meant to pay the man.

He drew five gold pieces from his pocket and dropped them into the fighter's hand.

Henney was surprised. He had expected more argument at least. He said heavily, "You're a man I could work for. If you need any help . . ."

"Meaning if I need someone killed?"

The man was not embarrassed. "Well they tried to

have you killed, didn't they? They'll probably try again if you don't get them first."

"They had Marc killed, didn't they?"

Henney hesitated. "I don't know." He said it reluctantly as if he hated to admit the lack of information. "The Hardrock Kid killed Marc. Pierpont trailed him down below the mill and put three bullets in him."

"He wasn't alone."

"The men who were with him lit out. No one's seen them since."

"And just why did you come and sell out to me tonight?"

"It's obvious, ain't it?"

"Perhaps." Hoe's soft laughter ran through the air. "But sometimes the obvious is meant to be confusing. Did you ever sit in a hotel room and have a man on the next floor drop one boot, and sit there, waiting for him to drop the second one?"

"Don't know as I ever did." Henney was eying him as if he had doubts as to Hoe's sanity.

"What would you think if the second boot never dropped?"

Henney's slow mind wrestled with the problem, then he brightened. "Why, that the guy only had one foot."

"The obvious, but there might be several other reasons. Maybe the second boot stuck and wouldn't come off, or maybe his foot was cold and he went to bed with one boot on to keep it warm."

The big fighter scratched his head. "And maybe you know what you're talking about."

"That's the point, nor do I know why my brothers wanted me killed. If you'd stuck to the Clayborne story, I'd have been more inclined to believe you."

"You don't believe me? Then why did you give me the hundred dollars?"

"Maybe I wanted you out of town, and paying it was easier than killing you. Good night."

He watched the fighter go, slowly at first, then almost at a run, as if afraid Les Hoe would change his mind. Henney was puzzled, but he was no more puzzled than Hoe. If Henney was telling the truth, why was it so important to Raoul and Clint that he die? Was it merely the fact that they feared he would cut them out of their share of Grandmère's money? Didn't they know what shape the mine was in? Clint was the manager of the bank, Raoul of the mill. Was it possible that Grandmère could conceal her desperate financial position from them?

Sleep brought no answer, and when he arrived at Clint's office at eleven o'clock the following morning Grandmère was already there, seated at Clint's desk, facing his two brothers.

His arrival interrupted a heated argument. Clint's face was somber, Raoul's a dull red under the shelter of the curling sideburns.

They turned as he came in, and Raoul said bitterly, "So you managed it. Clint and I sweat for ten years to build up the family fortune, and you, almost a stranger, walk in and take over."

He glanced at them and then at Grandmère. Her face this morning was smooth, impassive, showing no sign of the hysteria that had rocked her small body the night before, and he remembered her words: "I can't let Raoul and Clint know what has happened, what financial shape we are in."

His tone was calm. "I talked to Henney last night." He watched for reaction in his brothers' faces. It was

60

inconclusive. Clint showed nothing at all; Raoul showed a gaping surprise. . .

His grandmother said sharply, "What's this about Henney?"

Les said softly, "Ask them," and walked toward the window.

Raoul stirred under his grandmother's gray eyes. "I have no idea what he's talking about."

She wasted no time looking toward Clint. Experience had taught her that it was seldom possible to get a direct answer out of him on anything.

"Are you two mixed up with Henney? Did you pay him to attack Les? Did you pay him to put the blame on Sam Clayborne?"

Raoul tried to bluster. Clint said nothing. He sat, his blue eyes partly hooded, seeming to watch both his grandmother and Les at the same time. She cut short Raoul's words, her voice as snappy as of old.

"You did. I can tell it by your faces. I don't know what you thought to gain. I suppose you had Marc murdered, too?"

No one answered her.

"Well, you fools. By killing Marc you played directly into Clayborne's hands. I'll tell you something I wasn't going to tell. We're broke, do you understand? Broke. Clayborne and his high-graders have ruined us. The only chance I saw to pull out was to stop the high-grading, and I knew that neither of you were tough enough to carry it through."

Neither Raoul nor Clint spoke.

"So you're through. Get out of this bank, and stay out of the mine and mill. From now on you're no relations of mine."

Clint said smugly from the desk corner, "You don't

own this bank any more, Grandmère."

Dull color came up into her face, her hands clinched, and she rose, leaning forward on her small fists. "I'll show you who owns what. Without me neither you nor Raoul would have even a dime. Who made you president of this bank? Who made Raoul manager of the mill?"

Clint nodded easily. "You did. But you forget, Grandmère, you sold your bank stock to meet the mine assessments. You don't own more than ten per cent of this place now."

She drew a long, tortured breath. She was not used to having anyone defy her, especially one of her grandsons. "All right." She sounded strangled. "I did sell my stock, but I sold it to Eastern friends, men who will do what I say. You can count on that."

Clint had his sly, secretive smile, the smile which Les as a child had learned to dread. He thought, he's up to something. He's very certain of himself.

Clint said smoothly, "All right. You have decided to trust Les instead of us. So be it. But let me remind you, Grandmère, that I'm president of this bank, no matter who made me that, and only the board of directors can fire me, and you are no longer on the board."

Grandmère fought for control. For a moment Les thought that she would charge around the corner of the desk and drive her small fists into Clint's smirking face.

But she won the battle with her anger and said in a nearly normal voice, "Come on, Les."

He followed her, conscious that his brothers watched them carefully until the office door had closed. Back in her hotel suite Marie Hoe collapsed in her chair, leaning back her eyes closed, her lips a little open as if she had difficulty in getting enough oxygen from the rarefied

62

mountain air.

"Clint's gone crazy."

"No," Les told her. "Clint never does anything in the world without a carefully thought-out purpose. The question is, what's his purpose at the moment?"

She shook her head tiredly. All the fight seemed to have drained out of her. It was hard to believe that this was the same woman who had whipped Carl Henney, the same woman who had ruled Two Mile with an iron hand, the same woman Lord Teal had dubbed the Queen.

"There's no way he can win. All he has is his salary from the bank. Without me backing him he would be nothing, nothing at all."

Les was not convinced. His brother had not acted as a man should when he suddenly has his world cut out from under him. "What about these Eastern people who bought your bank stock? Who are they? Who arranged the sale?"

"Marc."

"Don't you know their names?"

"I was so busy." She said it defensively. "Marc found the buyers. They'll be listed on the bank-stock books."

"Which Clint has, and which I doubt that he'll let us see."

She stared at him, a little helplessly. "But we need that bank. I've managed through the years to keep other banks from starting in Two Mile. Recently we've been forced to borrow our payroll against our gold shipments. It takes thirty to sixty days to get money from the Denver mint, and the bank advances the money to the mining company."

"And if we don't get it?"

She said flatly, "We don't meet next week's payroll."

Les Hoe had a sudden crushing realization that he knew very little about business, that he was not competent to meet the situation. Business had always appeared fairly simple to him; a man hired other men to do things, and sold the product of their labor, and paid their wages out of what he got for it.

When you came to borrowing money to meet a payroll, giving mint receipts as collateral, this was something outside his experience. Grandmère knew how such things worked, but Grandmère was no longer thinking clearly. He said, "How about the banks in Denver?"

Her eyes were bleak. "Banks like financial statements and earning reports. As long as the high-graders keep robbing us blind, our operation would not be considered a good banking risk."

"Then the first thing is to stop the high-grading." He turned toward the door, but her voice halted him.

"Les."

He turned.

"Take care of yourself. If anything happens to you I don't know what I'd do. I'm too old to do it alone."

CHAPTER 8

AFTER THE OFFICE DOOR CLOSED BEHIND LES AND their grandmother, Raoul said nervously, "Was it wise to make an open break?"

Clint watched him. Clint thought, as he had a hundred times before, how odd it was that a family could produce so shrewd a person as he accounted himself to be and at the same time a pompous fool like Raoul.

Still, Raoul had been of value as a willing tool, never

actually questioning his operations as long as there was enough money to support the greedy women who hung around him.

He said, "The mistake we made was in trying to kill Les. I admit that I panicked when he first came here. I pictured him as a hell-for-leather killer who would go for his gun as soon as he discovered anything odd. I was wrong. I've never seen a meeker person. I doubt that he would fight if you rubbed his nose in the dirt."

"He handled Henney."

"Oh, he knows how to handle himself. He'd never have made his reputation if he hadn't, but that isn't my point. As far as being any actual danger to us is concerned, he isn't. In fact, I think he'll turn out to be an advantage."

Raoul's face was clouded by doubt, and Clint chuckled. "You never can see things until they're explained to you, can you?"

Raoul turned sullen, as he always did when his brother's sharper tongue lashed him. "What do you mean?"

Clint Hoe said slowly, "What do you think Les Hoe's first move will be?"

"To put in change rooms."

"Exactly, and what will the miners do?"

"They won't like it."

Clint laughed louder than usual. "That, my thick-headed brother, is the understatement of the year. Of course they won't like it. Would you like it if you'd,been stealing a hundred dollars a day and suddenly you can't make more than four?"

"And the Claybornes won't like it, bless their thieving souls. There'll be no more stolen ore for them to buy. They can't run their mill on their own pitiful mine, so the Judge will make a fiery speech and the miners will go out on strike and close the mines."

Raoul stared at him. Raoul might not be the smartest person in the world, but he knew that for the last two years he and Clint had been stealing Grandmére blind.

The plan was simple, as all profitable criminal operations are. Men in Clint's employ sorted the ore underground, sacking the high-grade in specially marked sacks when they went to the mill. At the mill, Raoul, by virtue of his job as superintendent, managed to switch these sacks for custom ore which was sent in from three dummy claims owned by Clint, farther up the mountain. It was easy to alter the books, to issue mill slips which were honored through the bank to Clint.

The idea had been born of the Clayborne high-grading, and they had used the Claybornes as a front, blaming the lack of mill returns on them; but actually, over a two-year period, he and Clint had stolen three-quarters of the gold that had vanished from the mine. With this money they had bought Grandmére's bank stock, taken up the mortgage which she had put upon the hotel and had nearly six million dollars in the bank.

The inauguration of change rooms would not affect their operation directly, but it would destroy the Claybornes; and they had masked their operations behind the Clayborne thefts for so long that he would feel naked if the Claybornes and their assay offices were out of the picture.

Raoul said slowly, "We can't let that happen. We killed Marc because he was going to put in change rooms."

"We killed Marc," Clint corrected him, "because Marc was getting suspicious. Marc didn't believe that the Claybornes were getting all the stolen gold, but we made a mistake. We thought that with Marc dead Grandmére would turn to us and we could take over the whole mine."

Raoul watched his brother unhappily. "And it didn't work."

"It didn't work." Clint was staring out of the window. "But supposing brother Les puts in his change rooms? Supposing the Claybornes stir up the miners and they strike and close the mines? What will happen?"

Raoul said weakly, "We can't steal any more gold."

Clint snorted. "It's lucky for you that I'm around to do your thinking. With the mines closed the stock will go down to practically nothing, and we can use the money we already have to buy control."

His brother stared. "Then we want the mines closed?"

"We want them closed," said Clint. "We want them closed as soon as possible."

He eased back into his chair and sat gazing at the window, not actually seeing it. His original actions had been prompted by a jealous resentment that Grandmére had trusted Marc fully while she had still kept a tight rein on Clint himself.

But once his stealing program was in operation and the money had begun rolling in he had grown greedy, reaching out for more and more, until his milking threatened to bankrupt the mining company. Not until he realized this had the final idea come to him—to destroy the value of the stock to the point where he could buy control with his stolen funds. When that day came, he, not Grandmére, would control the mine, and thus the town.

Marc had been in his way, and he had paid to have him killed. Les seemed to offer a danger, and he had paid Carl Henney to remove him; but sitting here now,

67

he was relieved that Henney had failed.

Better this way. Let his younger brother install change rooms, let the miners strike and close the mine. Let it stay closed until the Eastern owners became disgusted and dumped their stock, until Grandmére was forced to sell her holdings for a few cents on the dollar value.

Then, when he had bought them all out, the mines would reopen, and the practice of change rooms would already be established. For he had no notion of sitting back and allowing the miners and the Claybornes to steal from him as they had done from Grandmére. Time was on his side. He had all the money he needed, safe in a bank he owned, and no one knew he had it; and unless Raoul talked, no one would find out until it was too late.

Clint's mind was as mechanical as it was devious. He always planned things with extreme care, and he was now charting his future, after Grandmére had been dethroned, after he was master of Two Mile.

He would move into her suite at the hotel, but he would not occupy it alone. He had already picked a consort to share his newly won kingdom—Sarah Baker.

The fact that he had spoken to the red-haired girl only half a dozen times in his life did not seem to him of great importance. He had wanted her from the first time he had seen her, but he had not made Marc's or Raoul's mistake in trying to approach her.

He had judged her and decided that she was cold by nature, that all she was interested in was wealth. This had been borne out by what Marc and Raoul had reported as her reactions to their advances. Money—that was what Sarah Baker wanted—money. And Clint meant to be the wealthiest man in Colorado.

He smiled secretively to himself. She was beautiful,

and he did not mind paying for beauty, and he expected nothing from her save a carefully arranged bargain. That would be enough. In his warped and twisted mind there was very little room for sentiment. It was not a matter of love. It was a matter of possession. He rose.

Now that the thought had come he felt a sudden desire to talk to her, to sit and merely look at her. He got his hat and set is squarely on his balding head. Raoul looked at him in surprise. "Where are you going?"

He had been so engrossed by his own thoughts that he had actually forgotten his brother was still in the room. He said now, "You'd better get down to the mill before Grandmére gives the order to bar you. Get all the books, and be sure that all of the marked sacks are dumped back into the ore bin. I don't want Les to find them there when he takes over."

Raoul nodded. He had not thought of this possibility. He turned and scurried from the room like an agitated squirrel whose store of nuts is threatened.

Clint waited until he was certain that Raoul was far down the thronged street before he came out onto the sidewalk and turned his leisurely steps toward the hotel bar.

A dozen people spoke to him as he passed, and he returned their greetings graciously. Long ago he had decided that the more friends he could make in the town, the better his position would be when the time came to take over.

Grandmére was arrogant, ordering others to obey. Marc had patterned his manner after hers, with the result that he had been thoroughly disliked by the majority of the town. Raoul was a buffoon, posturing, preening himself for the dance-hall girls and other female friends he gathered around him.

But Clint knew that when his name was mentioned it was usually with respect.

He reached the entrance and stepped inside, moving quietly to the crowded bar, speaking kindly to the men who shifted to make a place for him.

He asked for sherry and stood sipping it, listening with a half-attentive ear to the talk around him, his eyes searching across the room for sight of Sarah Baker. She was not at any of the layouts, and he replaced his half-empty glass on the counter and moved unobtrusively to the door of her office.

In answer to his knock he heard her husky voice, and pushed open the door to see her at her littered desk. "May I come in for a minute?"

Sarah Baker was startled, but none of the surprise showed in the emotionless mask of her face. Had it been Raoul she would have ordered him away, for his pompousness annoyed her. But her relationship with Clint had been of the slightest, and she felt a real curiosity where he was concerned.

She was too shrewd not to sense the guile within him and she was never quite certain what he was about. "Come in," she said, and watched him enter, and close the door, and carefully remove his hat before he crossed to sink, a little self-consciously, into the seat beside her desk.

Watching him, she wondered what was on his mind, what had prompted his visit, what he was after, for she was fully convinced that Clint Hoe never did anything without careful thought. "Can I help you?"

He said slowly, "I understand you're a friend of my brother Les?"

At once she was on her guard. She said easily, "I know him, yes. I was in Deadwood, so was he. I know

70

Pierpont for the same reasons. It's wise for a gambling-house owner to be friendly with the marshal."

He considered this. It fitted well with the picture of her he had formed in his mind, and he thought, "This is the proper woman for me. Once I can trust her, once she can understand exactly what I am, we can go far together."

Aloud he said, "I know that my brothers Marc and Raoul have caused you a certain annoyance. Believe me, I'll never make that mistake."

She did not speak. In the years since she had run gambling saloons Sarah Baker had met many men. For her own protection she had studied them, analyzing their motives and approaches.

Clint confused her, but she knew he was not there by chance. He wanted something, and she meant to find out what it was. She said briskly, "You are a busy man, an important man, not a man who wastes time. Can I help you?"

He smiled. "You can have dinner with me."

This was the last thing she had expected, and it was all she could do to conceal her start of surprise. She had consistently refused any invitation from a man during the long lonely years since she had put her husband into a sanitarium, and she was about to refuse now, but his next words stopped her.

"There are going to be some changes in Two Mile. I wouldn't tell you if I didn't realize that you were closemouthed, but the day when my grandmother cracks the whip is over."

She looked at him inquiringly, and he smirked. "Everyone has always believed that I was unimportant beside Marc and Grandmére. Well, the time is coming when they'll realize how wrong they were."

71

She watched him. She had no interest in Marie Hoe or her affairs, but she was desperately interested in Les Hoe and anything that might affect him.

The supper invitation which she had been about to reject offered an opening where she might exploit Clint's apparent willingness to talk.

"I usually eat about eight. I have to be back here at nine-thirty."

A wave of confidence swept through Clint Hoe. He had hesitated over this step a long time, and it had been so easy. This girl was as smart as he had thought. She realized that of all the family, he offered her the greatest chance of advancement.

"Fine." He rose. "Shall I pick you up here?"

"At my rooms," she said, referring to the suite which she occupied on the second floor of the hotel. "Say at seven-thirty."

She watched him leave, thinking that from the way he walked he might have been striding on air. Then she sat at her desk, her eyes on the pile of papers, without seeing them. Finally she rose and moved out into the gambling room, motioning to one of the floor men she trusted.

"Do you know what Les Hoe looks like?"

He nodded. "Everyone in town does, I think."

"Find him. Tell him it's important. I want to talk to him before tonight."

CHAPTER 9

LES HOE WAS SEARCHING FOR A MAN NAMED O'SHEA. He had no idea what he looked like, or where he might be found, but he went on the assumption that everyone in Two Mile must be known to at least one bartender. He had reached the twelfth saloon before he struck pay dirt, and at first the bartender was not anxious to talk.

"You're Les Hoe," he said. "What would you be wanting with Shamus O'Shea?"

Les grinned, sizing up the man. He had a broad Irish face, a bent nose and battered lips.

"No harm," he said. "That I promise you."

The man scratched a misshapen ear with a none-too-clean forefinger. "I guess Shamus can take care of himself, even with you. He's been in trouble ever since I've known him, which is quite a long spell, seeing we were born in the same house in old Dublin."

"Would you know where he is now?"

"I know where he lives, but that's no sign that he's there."

"And where would that be?"

The bartender directed him to a miners' boardinghouse on Park. He climbed the sloping steps, knocked, and a large Cornish woman with orange hair answered his knock, staring at him with unveiled hostility.

"We'ns want nothing, naught at all."

He said, "I'm looking for Shamus O'Shea."

"And what would you be wanting with himself?"

"To talk, that's all."

"Coo, and there's no one in the world can talk to O'Shea, for he'll do all the talking himself. You'll not talk to him this day, for he rode out to argue the rights of the Irish war with Lord Teal."

Hoe thanked her and went back down the steps. At the livery he rented a hammer-headed roan with a mean eye and rode down the winding canyon trail toward the White Boar's Head Inn.

His progress was slowed by the heavy freight wagons, forming an almost continuous line as they moved slowly upward, bringing their loads from far-off Denver. It was well along in the afternoon before he turned his horse into the innyard, stepped down, tied him to the corral fence, and moved toward the taproom door.

Actually less than two days had elapsed since he had ridden up this road on the swaying top of the stage, but so much had happened that he felt he had been in this canyon a year.

There were only two people in the barroom—Lord Teal behind the rough counter and a tall, cadaverous man with lank black hair and deep-set burning eyes facing him. They were arguing as Les Hoe entered, and he heard the tall man say, "Where would Wellington have been without his Irish regiments? How would the British Empire have survived without the misguided sons of Erin fighting her battles on land and sea?"

Teal laughed. "O'Shea, you're a fool, and I'm a fool. You were driven out of Ireland, and I was run out of England. We're both a couple of blackguards, and you know it."

"That has absolutely nothing to do with it." O'Shea used his beer mug to pound the bar. "You're evading the issue as usual. The point is . . ." He stopped, becoming conscious of Les Hoe's presence, and turned. Teal looked up and also saw Hoe and nodded a welcome.

"Hi, Marshal. I trust you aren't leaving the country so soon."

Les moved forward to the bar to stand at O'Shea's side. "Not quite yet. I rode out looking for a man named O'Shea."

"You're looking right at him," Teal said. "And I

74

would thank you if you would take him away from here. He's a damn blabbermouth Irishman, and he wastes my time."

O'Shea examined Hoe candidly, as some kind of rare specimen he found interesting. "So, you're the killer marshal of Deadwood. I've seen you on the street, but up until this moment I've been fortunate enough not to meet you."

Hoe grinned, and the grin only seemed to inflame the Irishman. "Laugh. Fools always laugh when wise men speak, but the day of retribution is coming, the day when you money-grasping monsters will fade from the earth and leave the wealth where it belongs, to the men who produce it by the sweat of their labor."

Lord Teal had busied himself pouring Les a drink. He said now slyly, "I have never seen much sweat exude from you, Shamus, old boy."

The Irishman glared at him. "It's a figure of speech."

"Everything you do is a figure of speech."

Les said calmly, "You can save the fancy words for your union members. I'm here to try and talk business with you."

Shamus O'Shea drew himself up. He looked like a haughty eagle, the proud way he held his head.

"Marshal, I warn you, O'Shea does not take bribes."

Les Hoe began to lose patience. Was the man as big a fool as he pretended? If so, he would be no earthly good to the Hoes or to the town.

He said sharply, "I never offered a man a bribe in my life, nor took one. You're supposed to be head of the miners' union. Are you?"

The black eyes studied him, then in an abrupt gesture the Irishman nodded. "That I am."

"All right. I know that you don't have too many

75

members."

"Your grandmother's fault. She has fought us tooth and nail."

"And probably because the miners are stealing so much that they can't see the need of an organization."

O'Shea's face reddened, but he said nothing.

Les glanced at Teal. He would have preferred talking to the union man alone. He did not know how much the Englishman could be trusted or how long he might keep his mouth shut. But Teal showed no sign of leaving, and without insulting him directly Les saw no way of getting O'Shea out of the barroom.

"All right," Les said. "We all know there's a lot of high-grading going on in the mines."

"There would be less if your family paid the men under ground decent wages. It's hard for you aristocrats to realize how a man feels when he is poor, when his family is hungry."

Hoe's lips quirked. The idea of anyone ever classing him as an aristocrat amused him. He remembered the river shanty where he was born. He thought of the salary he had drawn for years. Certainly two hundred dollars a month was not an aristocratic income.

He said softly "And what would you consider a fair wage?"

The question caught the Irishman off balance. He pulled his long underlip thoughtfully "We've been asking for seven dollars a day."

"But you didn't expect to get it. Come on, I'm trying to talk sense. Never mind your trick phrases. What do you want?"

O'Shea was not used to facing up to things quite so abruptly "Well, say six."

"All right. The base wage at the Consolidated will be

76

six dollars a day from now on, with a bonus for every face crew that digs a third more ore than has been standard in the last year, a bonus of two dollars."

O'Shea got a dazed look On his narrow face. Lord Teal stared openly.

"The Queen will never stand for that."

Les Hoe glanced toward him and said roughly, "The Queen has nothing to do with it. I'm running things from now on."

The labor leader caught his breath, and his eyes turned hungry. Then he laughed shortly. "You don't mean it, or if you do, you want something."

Hoe nodded. "I want something."

"What?"

"I'm not good at making speeches like you are, and I don't know a lot of words that may mean a couple of different things. I'll lay my cards on the table. The high-grading has got to stop. For your information, although I'd rather you did not repeat it, the mining company is broke."

They gaped. If he had told them suddenly that Rock Mountain had vanished overnight they could not have been more surprised.

"Broke?" It was Lord Teal. "You're joking, man."

"Do I look like I'm joking?"

Teal said, "But that's impossible. The mines are as rich as any in Colorado."

"And the miners are carrying away all the ore that's really fit to mill."

Suddenly O'Shea laughed, a bitter, mocking laugh. "I might have known. You offer wages, and you admit you are broke. What good is the promise of wages if you can't pay?"

Hoe said steadily, "That's the point. If the mines

close, who will suffer?"

"The Queen, you, your brothers."

"That's right, but we aren't going to starve. We managed to live before the mines were open, and we'll probably live long after they close. But what about the town, what about the seven thousand miners you're supposed to represent?"

"What?"

It was obvious that this aspect of the situation had not occurred to the Irishman.

"If the mines close, the town will die, and your workers will be out of jobs, forced to move away. It seems to me that a forward-looking labor group would be just as interested in seeing that the business which pays their wages survives as are the owners."

It was a new concept, one which O'Shea turned over and over in his mind. It was a long while before he nodded. "You're right," he said slowly. Then as the meaning of the idea spread across his consciousness, he added, "You're right. Any labor movement to be effective must be a kind of partner with the owners."

Hoe waited.

"And you want me to stop the high-grading." O'Shea's face turned sour. He said with a kind of helplessness, "With less than a thousand members, a thousand out of seven I'm afraid I can't help you there."

"I'll stop the high-grading," Hoe said with confidence

"Stop it how?"

"Change rooms. Seeing that no man coming off shift carries out ore in his clothes."

O'Shea grunted. "Then what do you want with me?'

"I want you to explain to your members why the change rooms are necessary. I want you to tell them that without the change rooms the mine will be forced to

78

close and that the pay increase I have just granted will never go into effect."

The labor leader sighed. "It's not as easy as that, Mr Marshal. You're new here. Listen, the Claybornes have been getting rich buying stolen ore, and they're not going to enjoy having the supply cut off. The Judge is an orator. He will try to incite the miners to strike against your change rooms."

Hoe nodded sharply "I want you on my side. I want every one of the honest miners to understand that the strike is not a true one, that no matter what the Claybornes say or do, I'm not opposed to the working man I've been one all my life. And you can ask anyone in Deadwood if my word is good."

They looked at each other appraisingly

"I believe you." O'Shea suddenly stuck out his hand "I'll call a meeting tonight. I'll explain to my followers. Not one man who carries a union card will go out on strike. That's a promise."

Les Hoe drew a long, slow breath of relief. He was not trying to fool himself. He knew that O'Shea spoke for a small minority of the workers, but at least his men were organized while the others were not.

O'Shea stirred restlessly, drawing out the big turnip watch he wore at the end of a heavy nugget chain, flipping open the hunting case.

"I'd better get back to town. Will you ride with me, Marshal?"

Hoe smiled. "Is that wise? You and I should not seem too friendly, at least until this is over. The Claybornes and the men supporting them are going to fight tooth and toenail to block those change rooms. They'll probably accuse you of selling out to me. It's better that we act almost as enemies."

"Got you." O'Shea's grin flashed suddenly, the first time Les Hoe had seen him smile. The man was a born actor, never so happy as when playing a part. "I hate you from now on. I will tell them that I wrung the six dollars out of you by force."

"Tell them anything so long as they don't join the strike."

He watched O'Shea leave with definite reservations. When he heard the pound of hoofs as the man ran his horse out of the innyard, he turned back to Teal.

"How trustworthy is he?"

The Englishman said, "As trustworthy as they come. Shamus sometimes fails to show common sense, but he's a dedicated man. If he sees a way to further his beloved labor movement, he'd die in the attempt."

"Let's hope it doesn't come to that."

Teal shook his sandy head. "I don't know. I've seen camps before where the miners got stirred up. A mob is never a pretty thing, and that is what you are liable to have on your hands when they hear about the change rooms."

Les Hoe shrugged. "We have no choice. Either they go in and the mine runs, or the mine closes and the town dies." He refused another drink and went out to his horse, taking the climbing trail which O'Shea had just covered.

He came finally to the lower fringes of Two Mile and turned into the mill yard. The constantly beating stamps made the air explosive with sound which could deafen a man in a few minutes. He left his horse, moving in to the superintendent's office to find the head bookkeeper in charge.

The man was small, carefully dressed, his rather fine hair parted exactly in the middle. He smiled, on Hoe's self-introduction, and said, "Your brother was here this morning, sir. He said you were taking over."

Hoe nodded and sat down at the desk which had been Raoul's. "I'd like to see the books for the last year."

The man blinked in surprise. "But Mr. Raoul took them with him when he left."

Les Hoe looked startled, then he said slowly, "Took them? What for?"

"I wouldn't know, sir."

The bookkeeper's constant use of "sir" annoyed Les. No one had ever addressed him as "sir." "Look," he said, "my name is Les, and I prefer that you call me that What's yours?"

The man was a little flustered. "Mr. Raoul always liked me to address him properly."

"I'm not Mr. Raoul, and the sooner you understand that the better we'll get along. What's your name?'

"It's Pete, sir, Peter Ashe."

Les gave up. "All right, Pete How good is your memory?'

"My memory, sir?"

"Yes, you posted the books, didn't you?"

"Of course."

"And could you recall any of the figures?"

"Well certainly, sir, not the daily balances, but the monthly statements. I think I could give them figure by figure."

"All right. Sit down and write out everything you can recall offhand. Where's the foreman?"

"In the sorting shed, sir."

Les went out through the mill He stood and watched. Ore fed down through the chute from the bins above onto the floor. Heavy stamps pounded it with their massive shoes, and then the fines, working down

81

through the screens, ran into the cyanide tanks and on through the batteries to be floated free by the pine-oil emulsion.

In the sorting shed above ore wagons were pulled up, unloading, one after the other, and he found the foreman, a stocky man of fifty, named Price overseeing the operation.

Conversation was difficult under the rumble of the stamps and Price led him into a small office at the side, where a clerk was weighing each wagonload as it came in, entering it on a slip.

In the office the foreman looked at Les Hoe thoughtfully as if trying to make up his mind "The Queen sent me a note this noon saying you were taking over, Marshal."

Hoe nodded.

"I'm not looking for trouble, and I m not trying to cause any." The man pulled a colored handkerchief from his pocket and mopped his forehead. "But I want to show you something."

He picked up an empty burlap sack, holding it out so that an X marked plainly in chalk showed on its side.

Hoe did not comprehend. "What's it mean?"

The man shook his head. "I don't know exactly. The high-grade ore, the better stuff, comes from the mine in sacks. The run of the mine ore is hauled loose in the wagons.

"For months the sacked ore we dumped into the crusher has been running so low grade I wondered why they bothered to sack it. Today, the ore I dumped an hour ago was the prettiest stuff I've ever seen."

Hoe still did not understand. "What are you getting at?"

"Why should the high-grade suddenly jump in quality? That doesn't make much sense. And there's another thing. We've been doing custom milling for an

82

outfit that owns half a dozen claims further up the mountain. They send their ore down in sacks on burro back because there's no road up there. Their ore has been running about a thousand dollars to the ton. Today the stuff I checked in wasn't worth milling."

Les Hoe was trying desperately to follow what the man said. The pound of the stamps partly muffled the foreman's voice so that he lost a word here and there; and besides, he knew so little about the business that what the man told him did not seem to make sense.

"You'll have to explain it clearer, I guess."

The man was getting more uncomfortable. He indicated the chalk mark on the sack. "One other thing I've noticed. The sacked ore from the mountain claims all had chalk marks like this," he pointed to the X. "But today the sacks from the claims were plain, while every sack from the mine was marked. If you want my guess, I'd say that for months someone has been switching mine high-grade for the worthless ore that came in from those claims. It would be easy enough to change the tickets on the sacks."

Les was studying this with care. "Who could do it?"

"Me," the foreman said. "Him." He pointed to the silent clerk. "Or your brother Raoul."

"I see. And who would profit?"

"The people who own the claims up the mountain. I don't know who they are, but the books should show. After all, their account was credited with every ounce of gold taken from that ore and shipped to the mint."

Les Hoe did not tell him the books were missing, but as he left the mill he was convinced that Raoul, and probably Clint, had been stealing from the mining company. The difficulty was to prove it. They had covered their tracks well. Without the books without access to the bank records, he would have difficulty proving it. He debated telling Grandmére and decided against it. Still he needed to talk to someone, and he turned toward the hotel bar.

But Sarah Baker was neither in the gambling room nor in her office, and when he questioned one of the floor men he was told that she had retired to her suite on the hotel's second floor.

He climbed the stairs and went along the hall, pausing to knock on her door. There was an interval of silence, then the door swung inward, and he found himself staring into his brother Clint's smirking face.

"Did you want something?" Clint's voice was mocking. "Come back later, Marshal. Miss Sarah is busy this evening."

CHAPTER 10

SARAH BAKER CAME FROM THE BEDROOM WHERE SHE had been putting on her hat before the mirror. "Was someone at the door?"

Clint turned. "No one important, just my brother." He watched her face for reaction and found none. He thought, "She has no time for Les, and even if she had, she won't waste a second look when she learns that Grandmére's money is all gone."

He took her arm, and they moved to the stairs and down them to cross the crowded lobby. Men who did not know who she was turned to stare at Sarah Baker, and those who did know her turned in surprise to see her with Clint.

Clint noticed the interest their passage caused and rather enjoyed it. From the semi-obscurity of being

Marc's assistant he felt that he was now taking the place which was rightfully his.

They came through the door, across the porch and down the steps, to turn up canyon toward Delmonico's. The restauraunt was the pride of Two Mile, boasting that anything could be found on its long menu that was served in the better restaurants of San Francisco and New York.

Antoine Ferrie had begun his career in the New York Delmonico's, and he appropriated the name when he first opened his modest place in Two Mile. By careful management and constant improvements he had built the establishment until it actually compared with the restaurant from which he had borrowed the name.

In an ordinary mining camp the size of Two Mile it would have been impossible for so extravagant a place to exist. But here miners were free with their stolen gains, entertaining royally either at the tables grouped around the raised platform on which a string orchestra played quietly, or in the curtained booths of the balcony, looking down across the protective railing to the crowded room below.

Clint had reserved a booth, and he followed Sarah up the broad staircase with the air of a conqueror, swelling under the attention which marked their passage.

Not only was this the first time the red-haired girl had been seen dining with a man in Two Mile, it was also the first time any of the people in the room had seen Clint Hoe with a woman.

Safe in the booth, their order taken, the curtain drawn into place, they sat at a table lit by a single candle and considered each other.

Clint bowed above the checked cloth. "This is the most pleasurable evening of my life."

"Is it?" She was noncommittal, again wondering what had prompted this invitation.

He gave her his sly smile. "I judge from your restrained manner that you do not share my pleasure."

"It's a little early to tell, isn't it?"

He laughed, trying to be ingratiating. "You are a true gambler, Miss Sarah. You never expose your own hand until you have seen the other player's cards."

She said nothing.

"This I admire about you. I can't stand most women. They become emotional. I would much rather have a girl who realizes that there is only one thing of any permanent value in this world—money."

In spite of herself Sarah Baker's lips quirked slightly. She gained control of her rising humor in a second, and when she spoke her voice was as cool, as detached, as if she were presiding over her faro bank.

"Are you by any chance proposing to me?"

Clint had not expected things to move quite so rapidly, but he was relieved. He knew that his manner with women was awkward from lack of practice, and he had not been quite certain how to broach the subject.

"That's right. You see, I have watched you carefully ever since you came to Two Mile. Your conduct, despite the fact that you operate a gambling house, has been above reproach. There has not been a whisper of scandal about you."

Sarah Baker was having increasing difficulty fighting down her desire to laugh. If she could only review the scene with someone who would see the humor as she did, Les perhaps . . .

Somehow she managed to still the mirth which bubbled through her and to say in a solemn voice, "Thank you."

"I believe in paying compliments where they are deserved." Clint was extremely serious. "You're a handsome woman. It is obvious that you have poise and breeding, which are qualities I consider essential in a wife."

She dared not speak, and he took her silence for hesitation.

"Miss Sarah, I can't expect you to decide at once. No doubt this opportunity is a surprise to you."

She nodded soberly.

"I do not pride myself on being a physically perfect male, but there are other considerations. I'm going to be the richest man in Two Mile, probably in Colorado. There's no limit to what I can do for you and no limit to what you may achieve as my wife."

"But your grandmother, your brothers?"

He waved a hand. "My grandmother is through. Her mining company is broke."

"Then I don't understand."

He said with a smirk, "I broke it, and now my fool brother Les is going to put in change rooms and the miners will close the mine. The stock will go to nearly nothing, and I'll buy it up for a song."

In another man she might have thought it boasting, but with Clint she had the feeling that he never made a statement of this kind until he felt the game was won, the cards in his hands.

She would have to warn Les as soon as possible. She was certain he had no idea what was in his brother's mind. The question came, how had Clint achieved this position? She meant to find out, and she set herself now deliberately to do what she had never before done, to charm a man, to make him believe he had won her so that he would empty his mind to her.

87

She would not have thought of doing this for herself, nor if Les were not involved, but she felt that Clint by his own shady actions had forfeited any solicitude.

She said slowly, "I simply don't know how you could manage it. The Queen is very smart. It would take a really shrewd man to beat her."

"I already have."

"How?"

A whisper of caution ran through Clint's brain, but his eyes told him that he had finally captured this girl's interest, that he had breached the icy wall with which she surrounded herself, and he said, "You will marry me then?"

"Perhaps."

"After you're certain I have the money, is that it?"

She said steadily, "You would not want to marry a fool, and certainly I'd be a fool to say yes until I understand just what you have done and what you intend doing."

He said slowly, "Will you do me a favor if I tell you?"

"What?"

"Allow me to kiss you?"

"Not here." She turned to glance down at the main floor of the crowded restaurant.

"Where? When?"

"When we get back to my rooms."

"All right," he said, with quick good humor. "I'll tell you then."

Sarah Baker was forced to be content, to wait. She sat through the long-drawn-out meal, wondering where Les was, wondering what he was doing. She pictured a dozen places, a dozen things. She tortured herself with the certainty that he was with Nell Clayborne.

He wasn't. He was at a miners' meeting.

He stood in the rear of the barnlike structure, the air around him warm and close with rising waves of tobacco smoke, the smell of many bodies and the fumes from the overhead lamps, and listened to Shamus O'Shea hurrah his followers.

The turnout was distressingly small. Les Hoe guessed that there were not over four or five hundred in the big room, but at least he had to admit that they followed O'Shea's every word with careful interest.

No one had seen Hoe come in. There was no one on the door, no one in the rear rows of seats. He slipped into place quietly, not knowing what effect his presence might have on the assembled men, and listened as O'Shea spellbound them first with the offer of a raise in wages and a story of how hard he had battled to secure it.

They cheered him to the echo, stamping their feet and pounding each other on the back. O'Shea held up his thin hands for silence. "Nothing ever comes easy," he shouted at them, "nothing comes for nothing. You have good jobs, you have just been offered fair wages, but unless the mines stay open, you will have no jobs, nor wages either."

They quieted then, the shouting dying out of them as he explained that change rooms were to be introduced in the mines on the morrow, as he drummed home the fact that if the miners struck, the mines would close, the town would die.

Rebellious mutterings rose through the crowd. O'Shea quashed them. "Listen to me, I say. Everyone claims that union labor is irresponsible, that we're a rabble of radicals, tearing down the business structure of the land. Let us prove that in Two Mile this is not so. Let us prove we have the good of the community at heart as strongly as does the Queen."

A man stood up in the front row. "What do you mean? What do you want us to do?"

"I'll tell you what we can do." O'Shea strode forward to the edge of the platform and stared down at the speaker with his deep-sunk eyes. "We are organized. We are a cohesive group. While we represent a minority of the workers, we know that each and every man in this room is honest, that none of you have paid a foreman for your jobs, that none of you are carrying out high-grade ore after each shift to sell in the assay offices."

The room was tense, excited.

"You have acquaintances, yes, friends among the other workers. It is up to each of you to be an ambassador, a field agent, to convince the others what will happen to us all and to the town if the mines close."

They stared back at him, so intently that no one in the large room saw the disturbance at the doors. But Les Hoe saw it from his shadowed place in the back row. Suddenly the doors were flung open, and a party of men sifted into the room.

They might have been merely union members late for the meeting, save for their number and their leaders, Sam Clayborne and a huge, heavy man dressed in a black suit, string bow tie, and wide-brimmed hat.

Clayborne marched down the aisle, the man in black at his side, his followers fanning out through the crowd as if they expected trouble, as if they had been brought along to handle it. Les estimated them between two and three hundred, and he saw that many were armed with short clubs.

O'Shea, attracted by the rising sound, lifted his head,

throwing back his long hair, and with a long finger singled out Clayborne and the man at his side.

"What right have you to break into this meeting, Mr. Clayborne?"

Sam did not answer. He reached the edge of the rough platform and, ignoring the three skeleton steps, vaulted to it. The man with him used the steps, and together they faced O'Shea.

Somewhere in the rows of seated men the cry arose: "Throw them out."

O'Shea said loudly, "You heard, Mr. Clayborne. You'd better go before trouble starts."

The man in black laughed. He had a heavy voice which carried clear the full depth of the hall to where Les Hoe sat. "If trouble starts, you'll be the first to feel it."

Until that moment O'Shea had ignored him. Now he stepped to face the big man squarely, looking very thin and very tall beside the other's bulk.

"You're a renegade, Bob Trask, a traitor to your cause and to the beliefs you once voiced. You have taken Clayborne gold, and I want no part of you."

The man laughed again. "And you're a fool, O'Shea. You always were a fool. Tonight you have proved yourself a worse fool than even I suspected. You are here telling these sheep what a wonderful thing you did for them, getting them a few cents' raise. All they have to do is allow change rooms to be installed, to submit to being stripped after each shift by company police, to be treated like slaves.

"Well, it won't work. The miserable handful who follow you may submit meekly like animals, but the vast majority of our miners will stand on their feet like men, fight for their rights which are theirs under the

91

Constitution. You, sir, have betrayed your trust. You have sold out to the Hoes and for their dirty gold tried to lead your followers down the path of dishonor and of shame."

O'Shea's Irish temper boiled to the surface. "No one tells me I sold out!" He almost shrieked the words. "No scab or fink can use those words to me." His bony fists knotted, and he charged the heavier man, looking for all the world like a scarecrow suddenly come to life, his elbows out grotesquely, his head lowered, as if he meant to butt the man.

Trask took a half step back and deliberately brought up a left in an uppercut, crashing it against O'Shea's chin. The blow straightened the Irishman, and Trask, not content, used a straight right directly into O'Shea's eye. O'Shea dropped as if struck by a single jack, and his fall acted as a signal to explode the hall into a battleground.

O'Shea's men surged out of their seats, thrashing toward the platform. The newcomers, sifted through the crowd, laid about them freely with the short clubs.

The result was pandemonium, everyone swinging at his neighbor, neither knowing nor caring which side he was on.

Les Hoe watched the milling, fighting men for an instant only, then leaped along the benches, heading for the corner of the platform.

The fight centered in the middle of the room, and there were only a few struggling men in Hoe's way. He was trained to handle such situations, and he wasted neither time nor effort nor pity.

The first two men he came against he merely shoved aside. They were too engrossed in their own battle to pay attention to him. The next couple swung to face him, and it seemed they would forget their own quarrel

92

and unite against him. He caught the first man's arm as it arced in a clumsy blow directed at Hoe's head and, grasping the wrist with both hands, swung him around and sent him crashing across the seats.

The second charged, head down. Hoe laced his fingers, brought the edges of his hands down hard in a rabbit punch across the bull neck. The man stumbled, and Hoe pushed him on down to land on his face, stepping across the body before his victim could rise.

He plowed through to reach the edge of the platform. Sam Clayborne and Trask now stood above O'Shea, who was trying to drag himself upward. Even as Hoe vaulted to the platform edge, Trask pulled back his heavy shoe and viciously kicked O'Shea in the side.

The union leader collapsed with a groan. Hoe could hear it above the noise of the riot behind him. He jumped forward, grabbed Trask by one of his beefy arms, swung him around, and drove a hard right into the man's heavy face.

Trask staggered back, off balance, to be caught by Sam Clayborne, who shoved him forward again, a hand against his thick back, shouting, "It's Hoe. It's Les Hoe."

It is doubtful if Trask caught the name in the confusion. He came in pawing with both hands. Hoe knocked them aside with his left and again drove his fist into the man's mouth then as Trask brought up his guard too late, he hooked a stunning left into the man's belly, feeling the grunt against his face as the air drove from Trask's body.

Trask managed to get hold of his shoulders and pull him into a bear's embrace, hanging on desperately as his gasping lungs fought for breath.

Les might have broken the grip, but Sam Clayborne

93

chose that moment to circle and jump on his back. The weight of the two men carried him to the rough planks of the dirty staging, and for an instant he was smothered under their big bodies.

Then he was able to break Clayborne's grip and roll to put Sam below him, Trask above. He brought up his knees in a jackknife and drove one into Trask's groin. The man howled, his grip broke, and Les Hoe's boots thrust him half across the stage. Hoe spun to his feet on the impetus of the thrust, and as Clayborne slowly rose, Hoe's gun hand dropped and he swung the wicked forty-four up to cover Clayborne's stomach.

"Stop it."

Clayborne stopped. Trask came upward slowly to blink stupidly at the gun in Hoe's hand. O'Shea stirred, and sat up, groaning.

Les stole a quick look at the battle still in tumult out front. There was no chance to leave the building in that direction, but there was a window at the rear. He walked sidewise, covering Trask and Clayborne, and reached down to help O'Shea to his shaky legs.

"Can you walk?"

The Irishman nodded painfully.

"Slip out that window "

He watched O'Shea cross to the window. The man moved as if drunk, rubber-legged, but he managed somehow to raise the sash, throw one leg over the sill, and slide down to the ground below.

Les stooped, scooped up his hat which had been knocked clear, and said pleasantly, "If anyone tries to follow us, they're dead." Then he crossed to the window, dropped easily to the ground, and moved quickly after the shambling O'Shea. There was a taste of blood in his mouth from a cut lip, and anger in his soul.

94

This he knew was just the beginning. He had no way of forejudging the end.

CHAPTER 11

IN O'SHEA'S SECOND-FLOOR ROOM AT THE BOARDING-house, Les Hoe helped the man strip and sponged him with water from the pitcher on the washstand.

The labor leader was in considerable pain, and he had difficulty breathing because of the bruises left by Trask's heavy shoes.

Hoe felt along the ribs carefully, deciding that two of them were cracked, and sent the worried Cornish woman scuttling for a doctor; then he sat down on the edge of the bed. O'Shea lay naked on his back, his eyes closed, his mouth a bitter line, his breathing uneven.

Hoe said softly, "Who's Trask?"

A retch of angry profanity broke from the twisted lips. "Used to be my friend. The organizer I brought in with me when we first tried to start the union. Then he opened an assay office and began buying stolen ore and I threw him out."

"What is he now?"

The dark eyes opened. "Don't you know? He's the mayor. He got elected last fall when he and the Claybornes wangled the miners' vote. I opposed him. They've been trying ever since to run me out of the union and drive me from Two Mile. They'd have killed me tonight if you hadn't been there."

His eyes warmed a little. "By gravy, I never saw a man fight like you do. You're a tiger. You have only one idea in mind—to win."

Les's lips quirked. "Isn't that the general idea?"

O'Shea took a deep breath, slowly, as if every time his lungs moved it hurt him terribly. "Some people fight for fun."

Hoe said, without humor, "The ones I've fought were usually trying to kill. So our friend Trask is mayor, and he's taking a hand in the game."

"Why wouldn't he? He's not only mayor. He still has his assay office, and he's gotten the other assayers together in an organization. Further, he'll have a lot of the merchants behind him and the Claybornes in this fight. They like the stolen money the miners spend."

Les Hoe thought this over in silence. O'Shea's voice increased in bitterness. "I've spent my life in the labor movement, trying to help the workers, trying to better their conditions. Then a man like Trask comes along and tears down everything I've built, and all he wants is to put filthy money in his own pocket. He doesn't give a damn for anyone except himself."

"A lot of people are the same way."

"And he'll lick you, Mr. Hoe. They'll close your change rooms, and close the mines. The town will die, and all these people will have to pick up what they can carry on their backs and move to another camp."

"We'll see."

O'Shea turned over painfully, his face to the wall, as if he could no longer bear to look at the world which had played him so false.

Hoe watched with somber eyes. "First time I ever saw an Irishman quit."

O'Shea swung back as if he had been stung. "I haven't quit. I'll never quit." His voice grew a little shrill. "When I was nine years old I shot an English soldier."

"Kill him?"

Slowly the man shook his head. "I wasn't such a good shot. I hit him in the leg."

The doctor's arrival interrupted Hoe's laughter. He examined the Irishman carefully, shaking his head.

"I've seen people who took less of a beating who were in worse shape. You've got a couple of cracked ribs, but they aren't broken. I'll strap you up and you should stay quiet for a few days, but then you'll be as good as new."

After he had gone O'Shea looked at Hoe. "You know you saved my life tonight?"

Hoe shrugged. "They weren't going to kill you."

"You don't know Trask. I'm in his way, and he'll wipe out anyone who's in his way. They would've killed me if you hadn't gotten me out of that hall."

Hoe thought about it as he returned to the hotel. He hesitated at the entrance to the gambling rooms, then turned and went in.

It seemed to him that the crowd about the tables paid him more attention than usual, but he ignored them, and after a glance that showed him Sarah was at none of the layouts, he moved over to the bar.

He ordered whisky. The bartender said in an undertone, "Miss Sarah is in her office. She said if you came in she wanted to see you."

He nodded and eased along the bar to the office door, knocking, and then opened it as she called, "Come in."

"Les." She was walking the floor. She came toward him now, relief lighting her eyes. "I was afraid I wouldn't get hold of you in time."

He looked at her taut face. "In time for what?"

"The story about the miners' meeting is all over town, how you beat up Trask and pulled O'Shea out."

"Oh, that."

She said, "It's more serious than you think. Boyce Pierpont was here ten minutes ago, looking for you. He's got a warrant for your arrest."

"My arrest?" Her words jarred him. "Arrest for what?"

"For forcibly breaking up a miners' meeting, disturbing the peace, carrying a gun within the town limits, and assault with intent to kill Bob Trask."

He began to laugh. "Now I've heard everything. I didn't break up the meeting, as O'Shea will testify. I was wearing a gun but so were a good half of the men in that room, and if I'd had any desire to kill Trask he would be dead now."

She said, "Maybe it would have been better if you had killed him. I don't think you understand the actual conditions here in Two Mile, Les. Your grandmother and your brothers in a sense ran this town, but since the election last fall the real control has been with Trask and the Claybornes.

"They've been content to let things ride along as they were. As long as no one interfered directly with the high-grading they were happy. But last fall's election stirred up a lot of bitterness on both sides. Your grandmother is thoroughly hated by the rank and file for her highhandedness, and the highhanded way Marc used to run things, and that hate is being transferred to you."

"So?"

"So Judge Austin was elected at the same time Trask was. He owes his place to Trask and the Claybornes, and if you're brought into his court he may well sentence you to jail, or even the territorial prison."

"Isn't there any law up here?" He was staring at her with bleak eyes.

She shrugged. "You thought things were bad in
98

Deadwood before you took over. They're worse here, far worse."

"Where does Pierpont stand?"

She considered this carefully. "Like so many law officers Boyce is in the middle. He owes his original appointment to your brother Marc, and he has always more or less favored your family. In fact, there are those who have called him nothing but a Hoe office boy. But since Trask came in he's been taking orders from the mayor and the city council, and if they order him to serve a warrant on you, he will."

"I see."

"What are you going to do?" Without realizing it, she had put out a firm hand and grasped his arm. "You've got to be careful, Les, you're surrounded by enemies."

"Surrounded?"

She said quickly, "I was so worried about the warrant that I forgot why I really wanted to see you. I had dinner with your brother Clint tonight."

"I know that, I came up to your room. Frankly, I was surprised."

Her candid eyes met his squarely. "I was surprised myself. I haven't accepted an invitation from a man in years."

"What did Clint want, or should I ask?"

She said tightly, "He asked me to marry him."

Les started. "He what?"

"It was funny. Actually I had difficulty in keeping from laughing. He began by saying that I was the exact kind of woman he needed, that I wasn't emotional, that I was thoroughly mercenary, that it was more a business bargain than a union of two people attracted to each other."

"That's the way Clint would picture a marriage. As

far as I know, he has never had a feeling of tenderness for anyone in his entire life."

"And he was so certain that he knew exactly what I was."

"You're a good actress, Sarah, you fool everyone but me."

She did not press him on this. She wanted to avoid that portion of the situation. She continued hurriedly, "He went on to tell me that your grandmother is broke, that he's going to take over, that he'll be the most powerful man in Colorado, and that as his wife I could play any position I chose."

"He's going to be the most powerful?" Les was watching her closely. "How is he going to manage that?"

"He figures that when you start the change rooms the miners will close the mines. Then the value of the stock will fall to nearly nothing and he can pick it up—not only the portion your grandmother owns. He thinks many of her Eastern associates will sell out rather than face a big assessment."

"And just what is he going to use for money to do all of this?"

"That's the point I'm getting to." A faint color came up into her smooth cheeks. "I did something tonight I've never done before in my life. Something I am far from proud of. I led your brother on, Les. I even let him kiss me. I had to. I had to find out exactly what he's been doing."

"Sarah, I—"

"No, I owe it to you, and to your grandmother who has been very good to me. It paid off. I learned that not all the gold stolen from the mine went into the Clayborne hands. A good portion of it, I'd say at least

100

seventy-five per cent, was not carried out by the miners at all. It was sacked within the mine, the sacks marked with a chalked X and hauled to your mill. There it was changed by Raoul for ore from claims further up the mountain, claims owned by Clint under a phony name. This account was credited at the bank with the mint returns, and Clint then transferred the money from the dummy account to his own."

Les was remembering what the foreman at the mill had said, remembering the marked sack.

She rushed on. "I have no idea how much he stole. You can check the account on the mill books. Maybe you can sue and recover."

"The books are gone. Raoul carried them away this morning."

Her mouth dropped in consternation. "What are you going to do then?"

He shrugged. "I don't know. I'll think of something."

She said, "If I could only help you. I've never seen one man so beset on all sides, and the tragedy is that you actually don't care about the mine or the money for yourself."

"That's right." He spoke slowly. "It's a strange thing, Sarah. Maybe I wore a star too long. A badge changes a man. But all men are not changed in the same way. Some of us grow arrogant we feel set apart from other men, we think our word is law. Others of us seem to gain a responsibility, a feeling that it's up to us to protect the people and communities, sometimes even against themselves."

"And that's the way it affected you."

He shrugged. "I don't really know about that. I'm not a deep thinker, Sarah, I only know that the Hoe family helped to build this town, they brought these miners up

101

this mountain, and the men are dependent on the mines for livelihood. I also know that it was my family who raped the town, who ruined the mine. What I can do to repair these things, I'll do. Then I hope that I never see any of them again."

She squeezed his arm.

He reached out and drew her to him, holding her shoulders gently, looking down into her upturned face, but making no effort to kiss her slightly parted lips.

"Sarah, few people in my life have ever gone out of their way to help me. You're as fine a person as I have ever known. I wish things were different. I wish I could marry you. No man could have a more desirable, a more loyal, or a more wonderful wife."

Her face and the V of neck he could see above the high collar were bathed in color.

"Let me go." Her voice was not steady.

He did not release his grip "I mean it, Sarah, if you were free . . ."

She said with a forced calmness, "No, Les You're being carried away at the moment, but even if I were free there's nothing for us. Don't forget Nell Clayborne, don't forget what she has meant to you all these years. Whatever happens, you and I must keep our heads. Don't let a friendship which I prize turn into something ugly. Good night, Les, and good luck."

CHAPTER 12

MARIE HOE HAD BEEN ASLEEP. SHE WORE A LONG flannel nightgown which draped clear to her anklebones, and her hair was hidden beneath a frilled lace nightcap; but despite the fact that Les had roused her from a sound sleep her black eyes were alert, her mind functioning like a machine.

"What's happened?"

Les Hoe stood in the middle of the living room and told her exactly what had happened that night, what he had said to O'Shea at Lord Teal's, what the foreman had told him at the mill, the outcome of the miners' meeting, and, finally, how Clint had taken Sarah Baker to dinner and what he had exposed to her.

She listened without comment. Marie Hoe had had the natural ability to build the mines, and she did not need anyone to point out a mistake twice.

"So my stuffy Clint is a fine embezzler."

"You don't seem surprised."

"No." Her voice sounded tired. "I've always known that Clint had certain weaknesses. They do not come from me."

He did not offer comment.

"How much did he say he had stolen?"

"He didn't tell Sarah the exact amount. I gather that it runs into millions."

She said thoughtfully, "I'd believe it more readily if it hadn't been for Marc. It's hard for me to think Marc missed anything like that."

"You're not doubting Sarah's word?"

"I'm not doubting Sarah's word. She is one person I would trust against all others in this world. Why don't you marry her, Les?"

His eyes turned uncommunicative.

She shook her nightcap. "It isn't normal for a good-looking woman to hold herself aloof the way she does. There must be some deep tragedy in her life. What is it?"

He said slowly, "What makes you think I would know?"

Her keen eyes were steadfast on his face. "I know her. She would never have exposed herself to Clint's pompousness unless she was trying to help you. Don't try and confuse me, Les. I'm sixty-five years old and most of my life has been spent studying people. That girl is in love with you."

He did not attempt to answer. There was nothing he could think of to say.

The old woman sighed. "You were always my favorite. That probably surprises you. Maybe because you were the youngest. Maybe that was why I was so angry when you quit us in Denver."

He said in a low voice, "I had to quit you."

"I realize that now." Her old voice was level. "I didn't at the time. I didn't even realize it when I sent for you to come and take Marc's place. They say there's no fool like an old fool. I guess I'm that. I struggled so long, and fought so hard, that things became important, and when the breaks started to come my way I got the idea that I was a kind of god."

He did not speak.

"You're right. I was wrong. You played it shrewdly, going to O'Shea."

He said, "I wasn't trying to be shrewd, Grandmére. Look at it from my angle. I've been a working man all my life, and I learned during my years in Deadwood that the majority of people, given the chance, are upright, honest citizens. I couldn't believe that the majority of miners were stealing from the mine. I don't believe it now. There is a certain percentage, yes. There are always a certain number of any group who are fundamentally dishonest. But the bulk of the workers

104

aren't like that.

"They may resent you. They may resent us because they figure they're not paid enough, they aren't getting their fair share. That's why I went to O'Shea. Sarah told me he was honest. That's all I asked. I know we can't win this fight alone. If we are to win, we have to convince the majority of the people in Two Mile that we're right, that what we're doing is right, that the only way the town can survive is our way."

"I wish Marc had had your vision." These were words he had never expected to hear from her, and he was warmed as he had not known he could be by her.

He felt a greater kinship for her at this moment than he had ever felt during his adolescent days. Who had changed? He was certain he had not, that it was Grandmére who was showing a more understanding attitude. And yet, it might be that he was looking at her through different, through adult, eyes. He smiled.

"I wanted to talk to you. I wanted to explain before I took any action which would jeopardize your property."

She surprised him then. "Say your property, Les. When I called for help I admitted something that I had not even admitted to myself. I'm through. I'm finished. I can look back on what I've accomplished without shame, without regret. There are few women of my period who have achieved so much."

"There is no one that I know of."

She said, "Save your compliments. I'm content with the knowledge of what I've done, but the fact remains that the whole business has passed out of my hands. The idea that Clint with his sneaking ways may scoop up the product of my labor burns more deeply into my soul than you will ever know. I would almost rather that Asa Clayborne profited by it than know that Clint had made himself into one of the most powerful men in the country."

Les was more startled by these words than by anything that had happened since he had arrived in Two Mile.

He said quietly, "I'll try to see that he doesn't."

She gave him a small, tight grin. "And if Pierpont comes after you, tell him to see me first."

Les moved toward the door. "You think he'll come?"

She said, "I think Bob Trask and the Claybornes will use every weapon against you that comes to hand. But I'm fully convinced now that the great danger does not lie with them. It lies in Clint."

He was at the door, his hand on the knob. He said, "Then it's all right if I go ahead with the change rooms?"

"What else can you do?"

"And supposing the miners close the mine? Supposing the stock goes to nothing and you're forced to sell out to Clint?"

Her grin came again. "Maybe Sarah Baker will teach me to deal faro. I'm sixty-five, but I guess it's not too late to learn."

He said, and meant it, "I guess I've never really appreciated you before, Grandmére. You did a lot for me when I was a child, but kids seldom appreciate what is done for them."

"Forget it."

"I'm a little late in telling you."

She walked forward then. She did something which she had not done since he could remember. She stood on tiptoe and put her old hands on his shoulders and kissed him on the cheek. "Never mind the mine." Her voice broke a little. "Don't even think of Two Mile. Pull out of here, Les, while you can. I should never have sent for you. Pull out, marry Sarah. Have a little happiness such as I have never known!"

He was shaken as he went slowly down the stairs to his own room. This was a new side of Grandmére, the human side.

Before, she had seemed to him a machine, pushed on relentlessly by her hatred of Asa Clayborne. He reached his door and, turning the knob, thrust it open. Like most frontier hotels the rooms were seldom locked.

He went forward, fumbling for the lamp which stood on the corner of the dresser, and then he sensed movement between himself and the lighted rectangle of the window and his hand fell to his gun, lifting it smoothly from the holster.

"Who's there?"

"Les, don't shoot." It was Nell Clayborne's frightened voice.

"Nell." He almost dropped the gun in his surprise. "Nell, what are you doing here?"

She came against him, and instinctively his arms opened to receive her, and he could feel her slight body tremble against his in the darkness. "Nell, what is it?"

She was grasping his shoulders as if afraid that he would vanish. "I heard about the fight at the miners' hall. I heard what Sam and Bob Trask did to O'Shea. I was afraid you were hurt."

"I'm all right. You shouldn't have come here. What if someone had seen you?"

She said passionately, "I don't care. I talked to my family, trying to get them to stop buying high-grade ore, trying to get them to close the mill. They wouldn't listen. They said you'd never manage to put in your change rooms. They said the miners would never stand

107

for it, that they would riot, that you would probably be killed."

Les Hoe thought of the number of people who had tried to kill him in the last five years and was not impressed. Still, he realized that he had never been pitted against anything as big as this. He said gently, "You've got to get out of here."

"Light the lamp first. Let me see that you're all right."

He found a sulphur match and struck it under the edge of the bureau top, raised the smoked chimney, and lit the wick, adjusting it carefully before he replaced the chimney and turned.

There was a long scratch down the side of his lean face, of which he had not been conscious, and a mark upon his jaw where he had struck the floor. Nell touched the bruise lightly with the tips of her soft fingers, suddenly filled with a pressing maternal desire to comfort him, to protect him.

There had been so few men in Nell's lonely life, and Hoe represented associations which ran a long way back. "Please. You've got to be careful. I think I would die if anything happened to you."

He looked down at her. Through the years in his dreams he had visualized such a scene with her, without ever really believing that it would happen, and now it had come. Now that he knew he had but to take her in his arms, to kiss her something held him back.

He did not try to analyze this resistance. His one compelling thought at the moment was to get her away before someone discovered her in his room.

"Nell, listen, it isn't fair to talk to you now. Not when you're upset, not when you've quarreled with your family."

She misunderstood, thinking his hesitation was only to protect her. "Les, you said in the shop that you'd loved me since we were children. Do you still love me after everything that's happened?"

"I think so."

She was in his arms, holding him tightly, raising hungry lips for his kiss. He kissed her, and in that moment knew a fierce triumph which blacked out all other thought.

"Nell, I—"

"You've got to stop them." She was speaking against his shoulder. "They're wrong, just as all these years your grandmother has been wrong. Together we can make them listen. We have to make them listen."

He had the picture of Bob Trask and Sam Clayborne on the platform that night and knew that nothing would swerve either man but violence, but at the instant everything seemed so very far away.

"Nell, you've got to go."

She nodded

"I can't walk downstairs with you. We must not be seen together in the lobby."

"I'll be all right. I'm not afraid. I walked around the streets many times alone at night. Don't forget, I've been raised in towns like these."

He said, "I don't like it. You go on. Leave the hotel and cross the street, wait until you see me come from the outside doorway, then go on home. I'll keep you in sight just to make certain you're safe."

She opened her mouth to protest. It stayed open, for someone suddenly knocked heavily on the door. Her eyes went wide and locked on his, and he flung a helpless glance around the narrow room. There was absolutely no place of concealment. There was no closet, and the spread on the single sway-backed brass bedstead was so narrow, it would hardly conceal anyone crouching under it He made his decision in an instant—far better for whoever it was to find her there than cringing under the bed.

"Who is it?"

Instead of an answer the doorknob turned and the door was thrust inward. As the door moved Les used his left hand to sweep the girl backward so that she was partly screened by his big body. His right hand lifted the gun at the same instant, swinging it upward, so that when the door was wide, Boyce Pierpont found himself staring into the dark barrel.

He started, and then was still. Then he said in a controlled voice, "Put the gun away, Hoe. I have a warrant for your arrest."

Hoe saw that there were two other men behind Pierpont and knew with sickening certainty that the story of finding Nell in his room would be all over town in an hour. But this did not show in his voice as he said flatly, "Don't ever open my door again until I tell you. I almost shot. It isn't a good way to die."

CHAPTER 13

HE SAW THE SHOCK ON THEIR FACES, THE SUSPENDED animation as for the instant their minds ceased to function, then, elaborately, making it a careful show so that they would understand, he returned his gun to its holster and thrust out his hand.

"May I see the warrant?"

Pierpont drew a folded paper from his pocket and stepped into the room and placed it in Hoe's hand. Hoe opened the paper, his eyes still on the marshal's lean, hawklike face, and took an instant to glance at the shirt-sleeved deputies who had followed their chief inside. Afterward he dropped his eyes and read the charges— inciting a riot, wearing a gun within the town limits, attempted murder.

His lips quirked cynically. "I've served a lot of warrants, Marshal. I never saw such a list of charges for such a little disturbance."

Pierpont said stoically, "I didn't make the charges, Mr. Hoe. I merely carry out the judge's orders."

"Of course." Hoe reached down, lifted his gun again, reversed it, and offered the butt to Pierpont.

The marshal didn't want to take it. Hoe saw negation in the man's eyes and thought he knew what was passing through Pierpont's mind. Had the positions been reversed, had they been in Deadwood, Pierpont would have resented the necessity of giving up his gun. The hand came out to receive it. Pierpont walked around Les and, pulling open the top bureau drawer, laid the weapon on Les's clean shirts; then he turned, his eyes gaining a troubled depth as they lingered on Nell.

Les said, "Miss Clayborne had just come to warn me about the warrant. She had heard about it from her brother Sam. She knows it's a put-up job, and she is too fair a person to go along with it."

He saw the open doubt in the deputies' eyes and had a sharp impulse to drive his fists into their smirking faces, but he realized that anything he did would only make the situation worse.

In a town of that size gossip was a rabid thing, especially when it involved a grandson of the Queen and the daughter of Judge Clayborne. Nothing anyone could do would be of avail. Nell Clayborne's name would be shadowed from now on until he married her, perhaps afterward.

He said steadily, "I'd appreciate it if one of your deputies followed her, just to make certain she has no trouble on the way home. If she has, that man will answer to me." This last was a warning to the deputy, and he saw both men's faces change a little.

Pierpont nodded. "Trail her, Andy, not too close." His voice also was a warning.

The girl went out, her head high, not looking at Les, not looking at any of them. Pierpont nodded to the second man. "Get back to your post, I won't need you."

The man went away Pierpont turned again to Les. His voice was low, contained. "I don't need to tell you I like no part of this."

Les did not answer.

"I have always been friendly with your grandmother and with your brothers, and I have admired the things I've heard of you."

Still Les did not speak.

"I would not serve this warrant, but if I failed men would say I was afraid."

That, thought Les, was the keynote of the lives of most men who wore the badge. Boyce Pierpont did not believe the charges the warrant made, nor was he friendly enough with Trask and Clayborne to knowingly play their game, but his pride made him face Hoe for fear men would not understand.

"Of course."

"As soon as I take you before the judge I'm turning in this." He touched the star pinned to his shirt pocket. "I've worn it nine years, ever since your grandmother hired me."

Hoe said, "You'll have another job as soon as you walk out. You are the head of my company police."

Pierpont blinked at him, then a wintry smile touched

his thin lips. "Hardly a place a sane man would take with much joy."

Les said, "If you don't want it. . ."

"Oh, I want it. No one in this town will ever say that I backed away from anything."

"There is one other thing," Les told him "I know how it looked, finding Miss Clayborne here. Those men who are with you, would they join our police also?"

Pierpont did not misunderstand. "So they won't talk?"

"So they won't talk!"

"It wouldn't help. Neither of them can keep from talking."

"All right. Now. Will I get a preliminary hearing tonight or do I have to sit in jail until morning?"

"You'll get a hearing tonight." Pierpont's voice was grim. "I made the judge promise before I agreed to bring you in. If you don't get the hearing I'll turn you loose myself."

They made a kind of parade going down the stairs and out through the lobby to the street. It was late, but the lobby still held two dozen people. It seemed to Les that Two Mile never went to bed. And it also seemed that everyone who saw them pass knew what was happening. It was the same on the street. They walked the dark sidewalk to the square building which served as a town hall, side by side, like two friends, but no one was deceived. Before they reached the building a small crowd had collected and followed them, trailing into the building and up the steps to the courtroom.

Judge Austin was already seated behind the raised desk. He was thin, with thin hair and weak eyes shielded behind square spectacles, a small-time lawyer who had been boosted to his present place by Trask and the

Claybornes, a little nervous at facing one of the Hoes, particularly the redoubtable marshal from Deadwood.

The crowd filed in behind them, nearly filling the room. The judge glanced at them nervously, then cleared his throat. His thin neck above the low collar and the string bow tie might have served a turkey buzzard, and his Adam's apple, which was prominent, ran up and down it like a bobbing cork.

Had the circumstances been different, Les Hoe thought, he would have been amused, but the stakes in this game were too important for humor. Judge Homer Austin was nothing but a pawn. Neither Bob Trask nor Sam Clayborne was present, but they controlled proceedings as definitely as if they sat in the front row with a gun.

The judge cleared his throat, glaring down at Les Hoe with a kind of desperate resolve. "Lester Hoe, you are charged with wearing a gun within the town limits, contrary to the ordinance against such action. How do you plead?"

Ordinarily Hoe would have pleaded guilty, since there was no question that he was guilty of the offense, but he could not afford to be locked in the city jail, even for a day.

"Not guilty, Your Honor, and I request a jury trial."

The judge fiddled with his papers. "You are also accused of inciting a riot. How do you plead?"

"Not guilty. I again request a jury trial."

"And now we come to a far more serious charge—assault with intent to commit murder upon the person of no less an individual than our honorable mayor."

Somewhere back in the room someone tittered, and the sound ran like a rippling wave through the crowd.

The judge looked up, his weak eyes angry "Stop it."

114

He used his gavel to pound the desk. "If there is any more disturbance, I will have the court cleared."

He glared down at them, and they watched him owlishly, like an audience that dares a set of performers to make them laugh.

For a moment he debated the advisability of ordering the room cleared; then, making up his mind to let well enough alone, he turned his attention back to Les

"You are hereby bound over to the custody of the marshal to be incarcerated in the city jail and held for trial, which will be set on the county calender."

Les said, "Your Honor, it happens that I know a little about law. I am entitled to representation by counsel at a preliminary hearing. Also, every crime of which I am accused is bailable. If you will be so good as to set the bail."

The judge peered down at him, and his weak mouth twisted in what in another man might have been a mocking smile. "You are very right to correct the court, Mr Lester Hoe. Since you are reputed to have served Deadwood well as a peace officer, I presumed you were sufficiently versed in the law that you would need no counsel present at the hearing. As for your bail, I was about to set it. Five thousand on the first charge, ten on the second, and twenty on the assault with attempt-at-murder citation. I hope you have brought the amount with you."

Hoe watched him with smoldering eyes. His impulse was to grasp the edge of the high desk, vault to the judge's side, and grab the thin neck between his two hands. If any man had ever abused the majesty of the law for political ends, it was this scarecrow on the bench. He would not have been amazed had Austin set the bail at five thousand, or even at ten. He still had enough in his money belt to meet that figure. He had never been a man to spend much money, and he had always been proficient at supplementing his income, since he had been one of the best poker players in Deadwood. Also, he carried his full bankroll about his waist; but thirty-five thousand . . . He had a feeling of despair. They were flagrantly trying to lock him away in a cell to keep him from inaugurating the change rooms, so that he could not save the mines and the town.

"Do you have it?" The judge was sardonic, thoroughly enjoying himself, and then before Les could admit his lack, a voice from the rear of the room spoke.

"It's here, Your Honor," and Sarah Baker came striding down the aisle, her red hair mussed, her face drawn hard as if she rode the prow of a many-oared ship, a Viking princess.

Somewhere behind her a cheer began. It swelled as she moved forward. Two Mile, for all its pretenses of grandeur, was still a mining camp, and in her own way Sarah Baker had captured the imagination of every man in town.

She was followed by two floor men from the saloon, each struggling under heavy bags of gold. They dumped them on the table of the judge's clerk, and the girl slowly counted them, a hundred dollars to a pile, shoving each pile in turn across the table top.

Austin was out of his depth. Nothing like this had ever happened in his experience. He kept silent as the gold was counted, until the last double eagle had been added to the growing pile. Then Sarah faced him, and her voice was knife-edged with contempt. "I'll have a receipt, and every coin had better be here when I come to reclaim my bond."

Austin sneered then. "It's lucky our would-be

murderer has such good friends among the shady element."

Les Hoe had had enough. He jumped the bar which separated him from the desk and dragged the surprised judge from his chair before he realized what was happening. Forcing Austin to his knees before the girl, he said, in a dangerous voice which could not be misunderstood, "Apologize to Miss Baker before I break your scrawny neck."

He looked up then, half expecting that Pierpont would interfere, but the marshal had turned, and facing the room, his hand dropped to rest on his gun as if he expected trouble from the crowd. It was unnecessary. They were standing on the seats. Someone started to chant, and the rest took it up joyously. "Hang the judge, take the old fool out and string him to a pole! Hurrah for Miss Sarah, three cheers for Hoe!"

CHAPTER 14

"YOU SHOULDN'T HAVE DONE IT." LES HOE SAT IN Sarah Baker's office. "This fight hasn't really started yet. I've apparently got my brothers against me, the Claybornes, Trask, and most of the merchants of the town, to say nothing of the majority of the miners. None of them are going to forget that you came to my rescue tonight."

Her eyes were grave. "What did you expect me to do when I heard that Pierpont had led you out through the lobby?"

"Exactly what you did. But I wouldn't have expected you to have that much cash on hand."

She shrugged. "I pretty well drained the tables. The

games are closed."

He looked at her and thought what a wonderful person she was, and his brow furrowed. Was it possible for a man to love two women at the same time? Only a short while ago he had held Nell Clayborne in his arms, and now he had the almost irresistible impulse to gather Sarah to him and kiss her hard.

She had put herself out of business in order that he might be free, and his voice was not steady when he thanked her.

She said calmly, "You'd have done the same for me. That's what friends are for."

That was it, friends. She must have seen the look in his eyes and was reminding him.

He stood up restlessly. "I've got to go. Pierpont is waiting in my room. I still have a lot of things to do before morning."

She glanced at the window where the early light was just beginning to gray the outside darkness. "You haven't much time."

No, he had very little time. He climbed the stairs, suddenly conscious of how tired he was. He was used to turmoil, but it seemed to him that he had been through more in the last twenty-four hours than most people were called upon to face during a lifetime.

Pierpont sat on the edge of the bed in Les's room, a cigar burning between his lips, his eyes focused on the patternless carpet on the floor.

"The company police aren't much." He was talking more as if he were thinking aloud. "There are only eight of them, and actually they're little more than guards. In a fight they'd be absolutely useless."

Les Hoe said, "You know the town and the people in

it better than I do. Hire who you can."

"Toughs?" Pierpont was studying him. "People like Carl Henney?"

"Hasn't he left town?"

"He's been hanging around Lord Teal's. That's where most of the rough element hangs out."

"Can you handle them?"

Pierpont said, "I can try."

"All right, recruit who you can. I'm going up to the mine first thing in the morning. Send the men up there as you hire them. You'd better try and get a couple of hours' sleep."

He watched the man go, then stripped, and, blowing out the light, rolled into bed. Three hours later he breakfasted in the hotel coffee shop; then he walked First Street to the edge of town and followed the slanting roadway which led upward to the mine entrance.

The original opening had been made in the mountainside a good thousand feet above Two Mile. This adit had been enlarged and was now used to drain the workings above it and as a haulage tunnel. The actual mine was reached from a vertical shaft, its head frame two thousand feet farther up the slope. From this three-compartment shaft the various levels cut southwestward to bisect the slanting vein which pitched at an angle of nearly seventy degrees.

Looking at the plan of the workings in the office beside the tunnel entrance, Lester Hoe saw that there were drifts at every hundred-foot level, and he was amazed at the size and extensiveness of the workings. The vein itself was some three hundred feet wide, the foot wall a granite schist, the hanging wall a kind of slate. The vein was a white quartz, laced with ore which

119

had been forced up through its fractured crevices by secondary enrichment.

The superintendent was a Cornishman named Jacks, a barrel of a man, standing only five feet five inches, and nearly as broad as he was high.

He talked, explaining how the ore was knocked out of the stopes by the blasting and sorted underground so that only the vein material was hauled out, the rest being used as fill for the worked-out slopes.

"They load it in the cars at the face," Jacks said. "It's pushed back to the shaft and dumped into ore bins. From the bins it falls through the chute to the tunnel and is carted out to the loading frame." He pointed to a huge boxlike structure to the right of the office, built on legs so that the ore wagons could drive under it and receive their loads. "Gravity is the greatest workman in the world. It saves a lot of handling, a lot of mucking."

"What about the high-grade?"

The superintendent looked at him with round blue eyes as cold as marbles of glass, and Les wondered how honest the man was and whether he had been a party to Clint's thefts.

"It's sorted at the face," he said, "and sacked. The sacks are hauled separately from the loose ore, moved out to the shaft, and lowered to the tunnel through the lift. Then they are again loaded into cars in the tunnel, run out here to the entrance, checked, and hauled in special wagons."

"All right, where do we put the change room, here or at the top of the shaft?"

The man drew his breath slowly. "You're really going ahead with it?"

"I am." Les Hoe's hard eyes met the man's squarely. "It's either change rooms or we close the mine."

120

"I hope you have enough help to handle it." The man's voice showed his doubts. "There's better than two thousand men working every shift, and we have three full shifts."

Hoe did not speak.

"There's an old ore shed." Jacks pointed out through the window. "We used to store ore there for shipment before the mill was finished."

"Let's take a look." They stepped out and crossed the tracks which led over the breast of the dump. The dump was comparatively small, since most of the county rock and bull quartz was now stored underground.

The building itself was some sixty feet long and twenty wide, built on the slope of the hill, its outer edge resting on the dump, its inner wall jammed against the side of the rising mountain.

Les studied it without comment. Then he turned to Jacks. "Get a crew in here and clean it out, fix the windows, and then build a fence down the middle. I want the men to come in this side, strip, hand their clothes to a guard at a break in the fence. When they are passed they can redress on the other side."

The Cornishman shook his head. "They won't like it."

"Can you think of a better way?"

Apparently the man could not. He went back to the office and gave orders to an assistant.

Les said, "Now I'd like to take a look at the mine."

"All of it?" The man was growing more hostile.

"No, just a couple of the faces."

The Cornishman shrugged and turned toward the haulage-tunnel entrance. The tunnel was wide enough for two tracks, so that the outgoing cars could pass as the empties were pushed back. The tunnel inclined at about a three-degree pitch so that the loaded cars ran out

121

easily. The empty ones had to be pushed upgrade.

Les thought that whoever had planned the operation of the mine had known their business well. As Jacks had said, gravity was called into use wherever possible.

Between the tracks a trench a foot deep and two feet wide ran nearly full of water, the drain for the mine above. They passed the entrance, and from a long row of hooks Jacks lifted down two miner's caps, lighted the lamps, and handed one to Les. Les put his hat on one of the hooks and adjusted the cap.

In silence they walked back through the tunnel, passing loaded cars being run toward the ore-loading bin outside. It was a good quarter of a mile to the hoist, and Les Hoe, who had never enjoyed being underground, felt pressed in as if his lungs found the stale air hard to breathe.

Jacks rang for the hoist, and it came dropping down, a big platform dangling from a cable. They stepped onto it, and Jacks told the operator to take them up to the six-hundred-foot level.

At the signal the huge donkey engine far above whined as the drum began to revolve, whisking them upward at a speed which made Les's knees give, stopping with a dancing jerk which he thought must certainly snap the cable.

They stepped out into the station. This was a stone room carved in the mountain's heart, a good forty feet long by ten wide. Jacks showed him the tracks where the loaded cars were switched and dumped into the ore bin to be shot downward to the loading hoppers far below.

Then they followed the drift to the point where it bisected the vein. The tunnels were not timbered, but here floor upon floor of heavy planks rose, supported by

122

square sets, arranged in the honeycomb fashion that had first been used in Virginia City.

Jacks explained that as the miners stoped upward along the vein, these platforms were built, the ore knocked down on them and mucked into the ore chutes and dropped into the cars in the tunnel below the platforms.

They climbed one ladder after another. The stope was already nearly fifty feet above the tunnel level and would go upward until it came within twenty feet of the level above.

Finally they reached the top platform, on which three men worked, drilling. One held the drill, the two men with the jacks alternating their blows as they drove the fine steel into the stubborn rock.

All along the face of the vein other crews were working the clink of their hammers echoing, their shirts removed, their upper bodies glistening with sweat in the glow from their lamps. Les Hoe counted over a hundred men in this stope alone, and the magnitude of the operation grew on him.

Back at the tunnel entrance he turned to Jacks. "I don't blame them for wanting money. I wouldn't work in that cave for a hundred dollars a day."

The man's eyes showed a look of surprise.

"But the high-grading is going to stop or the mine will be closed." He turned as a group of men came slowly up the mine road from the end of Two Mile's main street, Carl Henney in the lead. He was startled when he made out the tall raw-boned figure of Lord Teal at the big fighter's side.

There were twelve men in all, and he didn't care much for their looks. These men were roughs; he knew it by the way they walked, by their clothes, and by the way they failed to quite meet his eye; but he knew that in what he had to do he needed men who would not back down, who would face up to the angry miners.

He felt caught between the jaws of a giant crusher. It was his first real experience in management, and he only wished that some of the miners could understand that he was fighting as much for their future and the future of the town as he was for his own.

He walked forward now, nodding to Henney and centering his attention on Teal.

"What are you doing here?"

Teal gave him a small grin. "Ten dollars a day, that's what Boyce Pierpont said. Right?"

Hoe nodded. "Right, but what about your inn?"

The Englishman's grin broadened. "You're hiring away all my customers. It was either close the doors and sit and starve or join the exodus."

"But the stages?"

"My Indian boy can take care of that handily. You don't want me?"

"Of course I want you. Where's Pierpont?"

"He rode over the hill to talk to the Bellows boys. They're tough, and there are five of them, but if I owned any high-grade I'd worry more about them stealing it than I would about the miners."

Les laughed. "I see Pierpont understands exactly what I need."

Pierpont did. He arrived two hours later, bringing five men with him. As they watched their newly acquired guards take their places in the improvised change room, Pierpont said, "I never thought I'd live to hire men like this. I've spent most of my time throwing them in jail."

So had Les. He said, "I never saw a more likely collection of cutthroats than we have. Think you can handle them?"

The ex-marshal of Two Mile shook his head. "I can't, but you can. You managed to build yourself quite a reputation in Dakota. I think they'll take orders from you."

The miners actually worked a ten-hour shift, but the time they spent at the faces was only about eight hours. Two hours were consumed in changing shifts, and the evening shift arrived and started into the mine almost one hour before the workers coming out appeared.

They arrived at the entrance in groups of fifty as the swaying lift brought down load after load, and the first fifty were met by the new fence which walled off the tunnel's mouth and turned them toward the old storage shed.

Those first out hesitated, then with angry faces moved toward the door. They were sweaty, dirty from their hours of work, tired. Hoe's new police, bossed by Pierpont, guarded the fence to make certain none attempted to evade it, and moved them along.

Inside, Lester Hoe greeted them grimly. When all fifty were within the building he told them in a tense voice, "This is a change room. From now on, every man coming out of the mine will remove his clothes, move to the gate, let the guards examine him, and then dress on the other side. Tonight, because there was no warning, any man carrying high-grade will be excused. Tomorrow anyone found with stolen ore is no longer working for the company." He pointed to a large box in the corner.

"If any of you have ore in your pockets or concealed in your clothes, it will be simpler to deposit it in the box now."

They glared at him, some sullen, some angry, others

scared. A number turned meekly to the benches, sat down, stripped their clothing and, carrying it over their arms, moved to the gate where Lord Teal and Pierpont gave it a quick examination and passed them through.

The others hung back, as if by delay they hoped somehow to escape; then as the pressure built up under the watchful eyes of Hoe's guards, more shifted to the box, emptying their pockets of fragments of quartz which were laced with gold.

But not all of them meekly surrendered. A big redhead, standing a good six feet four, crossed to confront Hoe. "You're not going to get away with this."

Hoe considered him. He said calmly, "Do you like working in the mine?" The room had hushed, and everyone in it was watching them.

The redhead had a narrow, wolfish face, and a swagger as if he liked trouble.

"Sure I like it, or I wouldn't be here."

Les Hoe said, "Without change rooms this mine will be closed within the week. It's all up to you, whether you want to keep your jobs, or whether you want to go down the mountain, carrying what you can on your backs. It's about time some of you realized your responsibilities."

The redhead sneered at him. "Talk. You're a big man Marshal, as long as you wear that gun."

Carl Henney had pushed forward along the far side of the fence. "Let me take him, boss." The heavy voice was eager. "Let me teach the clown some sense."

Les ignored him. He said to the redhead, but he was speaking to the room, "If I lick you, will the rest of you strip and pass through that gate quietly?"

Someone laughed. Apparently the redhead was noted as a fighter. "And what if I win?"

Les Hoe appraised him thoughtfully. The man

126

outweighed him thirty pounds; he had height and reach, but there was a clumsiness in the way he moved and he looked musclebound from his years of swinging a jackhammer.

Slowly Les unfastened his belt and passed the gun across the fence to Boyce Pierpont. "If anyone tries to interfere, shoot him."

Pierpont grunted, not approving, but Hoe paid no attention to him. He swung back to face the redhead. "If you lick me, the change room goes out. If I lick you, the rest of the men go through without argument. Right?,"

The redhead grinned suddenly, and then laughed, swinging about to check the miners grouped behind him. "Right."

A yell rang through the big room. "Take him, Saunders. Take him." It was obvious that the redhead was popular, a kind of leader; that they had full confidence in his ability to demolish Hoe.

Red Saunders peeled off his shirt. As he did so a dozen small pieces of high-grade which had been concealed beneath fell to the floor, and laughter again filled the big room.

Without the shirt the man looked even more impressive. He stood enormous, and the muscles rippled along his back when he flexed his arms.

Hoe measured him calmly, deliberately, like a woodsman studying a tree he is about to fell. He was a trained fighter, trained to one purpose only, to disable his opponent, but standing there, he felt some of his confidence wash out of him. If those powerful arms ever tightened about him they could snap his spine like a glass stem.

CHAPTER 15

SAUNDERS CHARGED, BOTH HANDS WIDE, BOTH HANDS swinging, making absolutely no effort to guard his long, pointed jaw. He seemed to hold the man facing him in too great contempt to make any effort to protect himself.

Either he had no science or would not stoop to use it against Hoe. Ordinarily it would have been a fairly simple matter to step inside the roundhouse blow and hammer the chin with either hand. But Hoe dared not get inside where the bearlike grip would close about him to squeeze the life from his body.

Instead he danced away, glad that the big floor of the shed gave him room to maneuver around his slower, clumsier antagonist.

One of Saunders' clublike blows caught him on the shoulder as the man kept coming in, and turned Les Hoe half around. He spun away, and as the man bored in again threw a right hand, high, which crashed directly into the man's mouth, pulping his lips.

Saunders backed off, shaking his head, spitting out a tooth knocked free by the blow, and Les charged, using the moment to drive a hard left to the man's body which made him grunt and, sending over a right to the cheek, opened a cut under the redhead's left eye.

Saunders grabbed for his shoulders, but the clawlike hands slipped as Hoe danced away. Saunders stopped, standing flatfooted, breathing noisily through his mouth. The room was a stunned quiet, the watching miners unable to believe that Hoe was still on his feet.

"Come on and fight." It was a grunt, forced between the mangled lips.

Hoe laughed at him. His confidence was back, riding

him strongly. If he made no mistake he could take this man. He knew it, and the surging joy with which he moved into a fight was back. He knew that Saunders also fought from a joy of fighting. It was something inherent in them both, that neither pain nor punishment would mar. In some respects a good fight cleansed a man, washing out the bile, the doubts, the torturing thoughts.

He threw a right; then moved in, sensing that for the first time Saunders was trying to cover up. The blow bounced from the man's shoulder, and he struck viciously in return landing his first solid punch of the fight alongside Hoe's head.

The force of it drove Hoe backward, and Saunders followed, coming in again, only to take another straight right to the mouth, a left which drummed against his ribs.

Both blows hurt. Hoe was an explosive puncher, his fists striking with the power of dynamite.

He lost count of time, he lost the sense that they were in the center of a room filled with half-dressed men. There was nothing in the world except himself and the redhead. He was gasping for breath. His arms had lost their buoyancy, were lead-weighted, and there was no longer the bounce in his legs which had enabled him to dance around the heavier man.

His mind was a confused blur. He had no idea how long the fight had lasted. Hoe knew more from feeling than from seeing when one of his punches smacked in solidly. He only knew, and this more by instinct than actual reason, that the man facing him was as tired or more tired than he. Saunders had put in a full shift, swinging a heavy sledge before his fight had begun.

The end came with the startling suddenness of such

129

things. One moment the man loomed before him, and they were at last standing toe to toe, slugging at each other raggedly, for all the world like two drunks.

The next moment his right fist crashed against the man's jaw, a clean blow, all the way up from his belt line, and Saunders went down, crashing like a huge tree that had been cut too far.

Hoe stood over him, rubbing his eyes to clear them of blood from a cut in one eyebrow, his lungs exhausted bellows, sucking greedily for air.

There was silence in the big shed. Slowly a small ragged cheer rose from the mine guards across the dividing fence. The miners stood silent, stunned, glum.

Carefully Hoe bent down. Saunders had struggled to one knee. Hoe got a hold under his arm and heaved him to his uncertain feet. They stood thus, staring at each other. Then suddenly Saunders' bruised lips split in a bloody grin.

"By God, you licked me." His voice was loaded with surprise. "First man who ever licked Red Saunders."

"You were tired," Hoe said. "Ten hours underground."

The man wiped his battered lips with the back of his hand and then spat on the floor. "Red Saunders never gave an excuse in his life." He turned to the staring miners. "Come on, you moles. Dump your pockets in that box and then strip."

They obeyed him sullenly. Saunders was still leaning against Hoe, but his amazing vitality was rapidly returning him to normal.

"You and me will have to have a quiet battle later on."

Hoe returned his grin. "No thanks. The next time you'd kick me for certain." He let go his grip on the man's arm, walked to the dividing fence, stepped over it, accepted his gun from Pierpont, and fastened the belt in place.

Later, seated in the mine office, Pierpont grumbled his displeasure. "Look, Marshal, that was a damn fool thing to do if I ever saw one. Red Saunders is noted as the best fighter in Two Mile. Not even Carl Henney ever licked him."

"I did." Les had washed his face, but it was still bruised and cut from the redhead's hard fists.

"Sure, but supposing you hadn't? What would have happened to your change rooms then?"

"It worked, didn't it? Every new group coming off shift heard about the fight from those ahead of them, and not one man has refused to strip. And everyone of them has dumped his high-grade in that box. We've recovered over five tons."

Pierpont shook his head. Les knew that the mine superintendent, also in the office, agreed with the former marshal. They thought he had taken a terrible chance. They thought that out of sheer bravado he had pitted himself against Saunders, anxious to prove that he was the better man.

He said, "Look at it this way. To these miners I'm only a name. Sure, I was the marshal of Deadwood and therefore probably tough, but most people resent law officers, and they also resent having to take orders from anyone.

"Also, you insult a man's dignity when you make him take off his clothes and search him, almost by force, like a small boy who's stolen jam or something."

"So?"

"But they respected Red Saunders, and by extension they will respect me as the man who licked him on even

131

terms. I'm still the boss. I'm still the man forcing them to go through the change room, but at least they feel they know me, they'll also feel that in some curious way I partly belong to them. Did you ever see a crowd at a prize fight? The winner usually becomes the local hero, right?"

Pierpont nodded slowly.

Les glanced toward the mine manager. "How many more to come out?"

"Five hundred, maybe. They should all be through in half an hour or so."

"Then I think the trouble is over. I'll go on downtown." He moved toward the door, but he had hardly stepped outside when Carl Henney came from the change room at a lumbering run, headed for the office. Hoe stopped, waiting for him to come up.

"What now?"

"Trouble. There's a man over there from the judge's office. He's got a paper. He calls it an injunction. It says we can't force the miners to go through the room any more."

Pierpont had followed Hoe from the door. He said now, "Austin knows better than that."

Hoe turned to him. "Better than what?"

"He's a municipal judge. His court has no jurisdiction outside of Two Mile."

"And?"

"And the mine isn't in the town limits. Never was."

Carl Henney was gaping at Pierpont, his dull mind trying to follow the words. "You mean the man with the paper has no business here?"

"That's exactly what I mean."

A slow grin split Henney's face, and his tongue came out to run lovingly about his thickened lips. "Brother,

I've been waiting to get a crack at that guy for a long time." He lumbered back toward the change room. Pierpont watched him go. A few minutes later they saw a man burst from the door and run down the twisting roadway toward the town below, shrieking like a Comanche; only a few steps behind came Henney.

Pierpont's smile was guileless. Hoe told him, "I'm going to leave you in charge up here. Break up your men into three shifts, so there are always guards in the change room. Put Lord Teal in charge of one shift, Henney in charge of the second. You take the third."

"You trust Henney?"

"As much as I trust most of the men you hired, but I think the worst is over. If we can keep the change room operating a few days, the miners will get used to the idea, and they'll be discussing the Saunders fight that long."

He saw by Pierpont's face that the man did not agree, but he did not wait to argue. He moved on down the hill, conscious as he passed through the crowd jamming the sidewalk that his name was on every lip.

He wondered what the reaction would have been if Saunders had licked him, and grinned ironically to himself as he turned into the hotel and climbed the stairs to his grandmother's room.

She sat at her desk and did not even look around after she had called to him to come in. "I hear you had a fight?"

He sank wearily onto the horsehair sofa and told her what had happened. "After the fight they walked through that change room as meekly as a bunch of lambs."

She tapped the desk top thoughtfully with her pen. "It may work, but I doubt it. Nothing is ever that easy."

He shrugged. "The Claybornes haven't quit, if that's what you mean. Someone got a court injunction restraining me from forcing the miners to use the change room. Pierpont told me the mine was beyond the town limits."

"If there's trouble it will come tonight." She was speaking almost to herself. "The longer the room operates, the more reconciled the miners will grow to it. Watch yourself. You're the key to the whole thing, and Clayborne and Trask know it. If they could eliminate you, I couldn't carry on. Watch yourself well. You should have at least brought Pierpont down from the mine. You shouldn't be walking the streets alone."

He shrugged as he rose. "It's almost as easy to kill two men as it is one, and I need Pierpont at the mine. Now I'm going down and see if I can buy Sarah some supper."

She started to answer, then didn't, and he left her, going to his own room to wash the stains of the fight away more thoroughly and then change clothes.

Afterward he descended to the lobby, pushing through the crowd which always milled around the tiled floor, and went through into the gambling room.

Although the games were still closed, men lined the bar. Half a dozen spoke as he moved by them. He nodded in return, hardly hearing what they said, and continued toward Sarah's door.

There was quick relief in her face as she swung to greet him. "Les, you're all right? There are all kinds of stories going around town."

"I'm fine."

She looked at his bruised face, at the cut which made an angry mark, at the eye gradually turning a faint purple. "You look fine. I'd hate to see you look worse."

134

He laughed. "That redhead has iron fists."

"He's a gorilla. What in the world ever prompted you to fight him? I never heard of you doing anything as crazy as that in Deadwood."

He explained again why he had fought the big miner, and she listened in silence. "It's a good try," she said, when he had finished.

"But you don't think it will work?"

She shrugged. "Bob Trask and Sam Clayborne aren't going to give up a good thing just because you licked one miner. I don't know what they'll try, but I'll feel easier if you stay off the streets."

"That's what Grandmére said. I take a lot of killing, Sarah."

Pain for an instant erased the beauty of her face, and she came forward to grip both of his arms, hard.

"Don't say a thing like that, even in fun. I'll never be really easy about you as long as you wear that gun, as long as anyone knows you are Les Hoe."

His arms had come up without thought, but she stepped away from him before he could close them around her, and after a moment he said, a little self-consciously, "I came to take you to supper."

She was about to refuse. He read the knowledge in her brown eyes. Then she changed her mind, saying, "I'll eat with you if you'll stay here. We can have supper sent in from the hotel kitchen. I often do."

He knew what she was thinking; by keeping him here she was at least keeping him off the streets for a short time, and his lips quirked, but he nodded.

He was satisfied just to be with her, to watch her, to note, as the lamplight brought them alive, the glints in her hair. He waited as she summoned an assistant bartender and gave him the order.

They ate slowly, almost silently, content in each other's company, trying to forget that outside the sanctuary of the quiet room the stirring pulse of Two Mile was beating toward a crescendo.

The meal was done, and they were sipping their coffee, when the door echoed to a knock. Sarah's face, which in her quiet relaxation had gained the peace of a child's, suddenly changed into the nearly expressionless mask with which she faced the world.

"Come in."

The door was pushed inward by a bartender, who said in apology, "Sorry to bother you, Miss Sarah, but there's a woman here insists on seeing the Marshal. She says it's important."

And then he was shoved to one side, and Nell Clayborne was in the office. Her blue eyes widened at sight of the table, the remains of supper, and the apparent intimacy of the people in the room, for Les had removed his coat and sat, leaning back, in his shirt sleeves.

He rose in catlike reaction, and she could not be certain whether his expression was one of surprise or consternation or both.

"Nell." He could not imagine her comming into a gambling hall, and the fact that she had done so, had asked for him before perhaps fifty people, would only add to the talk about them which had started when she had been discovered in his room the night before.

"Nell, what on earth are you doing here?"

She was blushing now, the red staining her face a bright scarlet. "I had to find you." There was apology and embarrassment in her voice. "The clerk at the hotel desk said he'd seen you come in here, so I asked the . . . the bartender."

He could have pointed out to her that she might have sent one of the bellboys to fetch him. He did not, for he realized that she would never in the world have entered this place except under the drive of a terrific emotional strain.

"What is it?"

"They've arrested O'Shea. They were having a big meeting. Father and Sam and Bob Trask were talking to the miners, telling them not to stand for the change room, and O'Shea and some of his friends tried to break up the meeting."

"Where is he?"

"At the city jail. I thought you ought to know."

He was already reaching for his coat.

Sarah Baker said sharply, "What do you expect to do?"

He shrugged into the sleeves. "I don't know. Send one of your boys up to the mine. Tell him to get Pierpont, to bring every man they can and meet me at the jail." He turned then and ran from the door, leaving the two women to face each other in wary silence.

CHAPTER 16

A CROWD OF ANGRY MEN MILLED AROUND THE entrance of the jail. Les Hoe did not know who they were, whether friends of O'Shea or part of a mob gathering, perhaps to hang the labor leader.

He shouldered through, just as he had been forced to shoulder his passage all along the sidewalk.

It seemed to him that every citizen of Two Mile must be on the streets that night, and there was a kind of sparking in the crowd. The least incident could make them explode. He had seen other streets like this where tension rode high, but never in a town this large, never with so many people involved. His lips set grimly. He was angry clear through, with a deep, corroding anger that twisted his insides and made them ache.

That Trask and Sam Clayborne had again jumped the labor leader lit a flaming sense of injustice within him. He had been prepared to dislike O'Shea thoroughly. Instead he admired him as he had admired few men, for he sensed the timbre of the man, his unswerving belief in his cause, his lack of selfishness or self-interest. O'Shea was battling for the rights of even the very men who had struck him down.

As he shouldered into the crowd, he heard the rising murmur his name made as it was passed from lip to lip and steeled himself, more than half expecting an attack. But he meant to fight his way into that building if it was the last thing he accomplished on this earth.

To his surprise, the crowd parted as by an invisible wedge, making a path for him, up the three steps and into the central hall of the building, and now the murmur rose, settling into a word pattern he could understand.

"That-a-boy, Hoe. Get him out. Make those bums stand in line."

He knew suddenly that these were O'Shea's men, the loyal union members, leaderless, yet standing by in the hope of helping their friend.

He turned at the doorway, saying, "Wait." He did not want them pouring into the building. In the resulting chaos anything might happen.

The men in front stopped, standing irresolute, almost pressed through the doorway by the weight of the numbers at their backs. He turned and walked into the marshal's office at the left to find, behind the desk, one of the deputies who had been with Pierpont on the preceding night.

He knew as soon as he walked into the room that the man was scared. He had faced down many men in his time; he recognized the reaction almost subconsciously.

The bluster was part of the fear, as was the fact that the man caught up the gun which had been lying naked on the desk as soon as Hoe came through the door.

"Get out of here. I can shoot you. You've got no right in this office."

Hoe stopped. He stood perfectly quiet, utterly relaxed, knowing that the least movement might trigger the jittery nerves of the deputy.

He said pleasantly, "You're new at this job. This is your first night as marshal, and it's probably going to be your last."

He saw the man's eyes jump and could almost smell the fear that rode him. "Don't threaten me." The tone was a kind of gasp.

Les Hoe laughed. He could not help himself. Not that he usually laughed at fear. Fear was too real a thing, too near the surface with every man.

He said, "I'm not threatening you, but there are two hundred of O'Shea's friends in the street outside. They're still outside because I told them to stay there, but they won't wait long."

The man glanced at the door beyond him. His tongue tip made the circuit of his dry lips, and his voice was strained. "Look, Hoe, I didn't ask for this job. I was shoved into it when Pierpont resigned."

"What's the charge against O'Shea?"

The man glanced around the empty office as if he did

not know what to do, as if he expected help from the bare walls. "There aren't any, yet. Trask is going to swear out some as soon as he finds the judge."

"You're holding him without charges?"

"I told you I didn't want this job. Look, I got a wife and three kids. I—"

"And I'd say that you've got into something you can't handle." Hoe's voice was still pleasant, but it had sharpened. "I never give advice, but if I gave advice I'd tell you to take off that badge, lay it on the desk, and write out a resignation, now."

His victim looked haunted. "Trask would kill me. He—"

"Go see Pierpont. You worked for him. He'll give you a job with the mine police."

He watched the hesitation in the man's eyes harden gradually into resolve. Slowly he put the gun into his empty holster. Slowly he lifted his hand and unpinned the badge and laid it on the desk.

"How do I get out of here safe?"

"I'll get you out. While you're writing your resignation, where are the keys?"

The man was thoroughly whipped. He nodded toward a ring hanging at the end of the desk. Hoe took it and moved into the corridor to the cell blocks. He had the fleeting thought that this was the tamest jail break in history.

O'Shea sat in the end cell, his bony legs apart, his elbows resting on his knees, his head buried in his thin hands. He did not look up until Hoe had spoken twice, and Hoe was shocked at the color of the lean face.

He had the grilled door open within seconds and was beside the man.

"What did they do to you?"

140

O'Shea wheezed a little as he spoke. "Just a beating. I don't think it did my ribs any good."

Hoe had a hand under his arm. "Can you walk?"

"Why walk? How did you get in here?"

"There are no charges against you." His dark eyes were as hard as anyone had ever seen them. "And the new marshal just resigned."

O'Shea straightened agonizingly. Every movement he made showed the pain under which he labored. "The rats, the thieving scurvy rats." He came to his feet with an effort and staggered out, and the cheer that echoed from the men grouped around the steps shook the town. O'Shea stood at the top, one hand on Les Hoe's steadying shoulder, and made a speech, afterward repeated and retold in every Colorado mining camp.

He started slowly, the volume of his voice building up as the emotion built up within him. He said, "Do you realize what Les Hoe did for me tonight? He wasn't too busy with his own affairs to remember that I was in a cell. The reason I stand free before you is because Hoe had the courage to come after me."

They cheered, but Hoe was not impressed. He had heard cheers before, and he had seen the self-same men within the hour turn against him.

He said quietly, "Save the speeches for tomorrow. I want to get you to a doctor."

"I'm all right."

"Sure, you're fine. If I let go of you you'd fall down."

He raised his own voice. "This man has taken a terrific beating. He already had two cracked ribs. I need a couple of strong men to get him to the doctor. The rest of you break it up. The trouble is over for tonight."

He regretted those words three hours later, for the trouble was far from over. It seemed that it had not even begun. Bob Trask and Sam Clayborne had rallied their forces when they learned of O'Shea's release, and they took over the town.

Les Hoe had to admit to himself that in all his experience he' had never seen anything like this. He stood at the window of Grandmére's rooms in the hotel and stared down at the main street. Two Mile was out in force, men milling in the roadway until even the teamsters gave up trying to move their loads and abandoned their wagons where they stood, the animals twisting their harness into hopeless tangles.

Hoe did not know what was going on. For that matter he doubted if anyone in the embattled town had the slightest notion of what was happening. Half the crowd was drunk, and Pierpont, coming down with a dozen of his men, reported that the word had gone into the mine, that the night shift had thrown down their tools and were thronging from the tunnel to join the rioters.

They had wrecked the change room and burned the mine office, driving out the mine police and the few employees who remained loyal. Now some three or four thousand of them were gathered in front of the miners' hall, and Trask and the elder Clayborne were haranguing them.

Les Hoe turned back, his face a grim mask. Grandmére sat unmoving at her desk, a wisp of a figure, resolute, all her hesitation gone. He thought with a rush of pride that Marie Hoe was always at her best when facing adversity, that the fighting spirit within her lived on opposition.

"You've got to get out of here," he said. "There's no telling what the fools will do, but one thing is certain. You and I are the two most hated people in Two Mile this night."

Her lips curled. "You don't expect me to run from that rabble?"

He nodded, "If you're smart you will. Only a fool stands in front of a rushing avalanche. It will take more than your ox whip to stop that mob, and you haven't a friend in this town, not one single friend."

She did not answer. Grandmére seldom wasted words when there was nothing to say.

"It isn't too late. We can get out the back way."

Her prominent eyes probed him. "Get out—you mean leave this hotel?"

His patience snapped. "Of course leave this hotel. Maybe I can slip you through the crowd. Maybe I can get you down to Teal's inn."

"That renegade Englishman." Her voice rose.

He said, "For your information, that renegade Englishman is downstairs at this moment along with Pierpont and a dozen mine police. They're the only thing between this hotel and the mob."

She said grimly, "I won't go. This is mine. I built it with these hands." She held out her small hands and closed them convulsively. "It's mine, mine, mine."

He gasped. Never before had he realized the depth of the fierce pride with which she regarded this building, the bank the mine, and the town. They were hers, and he sensed that she would rather die than ever let them go.

"What if they burn the place?"

"Burn?" She flung a look at him. "Burn? Oh no." There was naked horror in her eyes. "Burn?" She turned slowly and dropped her head, burying it in her crossed arms.

CHAPTER 17

CLINT HOE AND HIS BROTHER RAOUL STOOD BEHIND the darkened window of the bank, watching the mob in the street outside. Clint, as always, had had a spy at the miners' meeting, and when the man had brought back his report Clint's face had reddened with anger.

But he held his peace until the man was gone, then turned to his brother, and Raoul was surprised to see him shaking with anger.

"The fools. The blind, stupid fools!"

Raoul caught his breath. "I thought this was what you wanted, the mines closed, the town shut down."

"Certainly it's what I wanted. But you heard what Renfield said. Trask and that old blabbermouth Clayborne don't know when to let well enough alone. The mine's closed. The men walked off the night shift, they burned the offices and wrecked the change room. Trask should be satisfied.

"But no. He and Clayborne are buying liquor for the miners in every saloon in town. And they're standing up there saying that the trouble will not be over until the Hoes are driven from town."

"But they—"

"Keep quiet, can't you? Did you ever see a mob once it gets started? It's easier to start than it is to stop, believe me. The next thing they'll be breaking into shops, looting. Then some of them will march on the hotel to get Les and Grandmére."

Raoul said cynically, "They'll have to take their chances."

Clint almost screamed at him. "You idiot. I own the mortgage on that hotel. I own this bank. I own a good third of the property in Two Mile. I can't let this go much further. After the hotel, who knows, some drunk will dynamite the mine tunnel." He flung away, the thought too terrible to bear, and hurried to Marc's old office. Raoul followed, and in the dim light from the window he saw Clint lift a gun from the desk, twirl the cylinder, and then shove it into his pocket.

In all memory Raoul had never seen Clint carry a gun. Direct action was the last thing his brother ever attempted, and he said in a voice mirroring his growing fear, "What are you going to do?"

"Stop Trask."

"You mean shoot him?"

"I mean make him listen." He half ran from the office to the bank's rear door and let himself out into the dark alley.

Raoul stood, undecided, fear mounting in him like a rising geyser. His dependence upon Clint was nearly absolute. For years he had hardly made an independent decision of his own.

He looked again from the window at the shifting crowd, and suddenly he wanted to get out of Two Mile, to get as far away from the writhing town as humanly possible.

He turned then, moving more quickly than he had in years. He went around the counter and to the safe, working the combination with trembling fingers. Twice he failed to get it open because of nervousness, but finally the heavy door swung back, and he caught up two of the sacks of gold coins stored within.

There was little paper money in circulation, but what the safe held he stuffed feverishly into his pockets. Then, not even troubling to relock the safe, he fled through the door and down the alley to the livery. He had a horse and was leading it outside when a crowd of drunken miners suddenly barred his path.

A big Cornishman in the lead grabbed his arm as Raoul tried frantically to climb into the saddle.

"Wait a minute." The man swung him down and around like a child. "Here's one of the Hoe boys, riding out for help."

A yell went up from the crowd. Raoul stood terror-stricken. "Listen." His words fell over each other as he stammered in his fear. "Look, I never did a thing to any of you, not a thing. Here." He reached up to one of the saddlebags and dragged out a sack of coins.

"Let me go. Here. I'll give you these." He thrust the heavy bag into the Cornishman's big hands. The man looked down at it, and in that moment Raoul spun back to the horse, flung himself into the saddle, and spurred down the slanting street. Someone in the crowd had a gun. The shot broke sharply through the night. It caught Raoul in the back, under the left shoulder blade, carrying through into the heart. He was dead before he hit the ground. He could not see them rifle the stolen money from his pockets and the saddlebag.

At almost the moment Raoul died Clint pushed his way into the miners' hall. The place was filled. Trask and Sam Clayborne sat upon the raised platform, giving orders, like generals, to the excited miners, their army.

No one bothered to stop Clint as he wormed forward in the press. It was doubtful if anyone actually noticed him. The air inside the hall was electric as Trask was saying, "All right, boys. I want twenty of you to go down to the hotel and get the Queen. No rough stuff. She's an old woman, remember." He grinned out at them, and his grin told far more accurately than his words what was in his mind.

"Bring her down here and we'll settle this change-room foolishness once and for all."

"What if she won't come?" Someone shouted it from the crowd.

"Smoke her out."

Clint had reached the edge of the platform. He jumped onto it, calling harshly, "Wait a minute, Bob."

Trask's fleshy face set. "Well, well, one of the Hoes crawled out into the open, I see."

Sam Clayborne laughed. Sam was a little drunk, not only from whisky but from power. He stood up, not too steady on his big legs.

"I've lived a long time for this night, Clint."

Clint Hoe looked at him. Clint was shrewd enough to know that Trask was the real force here. None of the Claybornes from the old man down had any real guts.

But Sam meant to savor his moment of power. He pushed forward, and Trask was content to stay back. "For years I've wanted to stand against you people." Sam was working himself up into a real rage. "But no, the Judge would never let me. He would never fight back. We've put you out of business, Hoe. This is no longer your town. It's ours."

Clint said sharply, "If you and Trask don't get some sense quick there won't be any town for anyone. At the minute you're giving the orders. Maybe you can stop the riot now, but wait a half hour and no one can stop them."

Sam shrugged, "Who wants them stopped?"

Clint said, "I do." He took the gun out of his pocket.

Both men started, for it was well known in Two Mile that Clint Hoe never went armed. But he stood before them now, his mouth pinched, his eyes narrow.

"Listen to me, and get this straight. You're going

147

down to the hotel with me now, and you're going to stop this riot. If you don't, I'll kill you."

Trask had remained seated at the plain table when Sam had lurched to his feet. He had a gun, a double-barreled twenty-five, tucked into his belt under the edge of his coat, a holdout. As Clint talked he edged his hand upward, worked the gun from its place, and now held it on his leg, screened by the table top.

He said mildly, "Put it away, Clint, before you get hurt."

Clint snarled at him. "One minute to get on your feet."

Trask shot him then, shot upward past the table top, both light charges striking Clint in the face.

The reaction of Clint's finger was spasmodic. He never knew as he fell that he had fired the heavy gun twice, that both bullets struck Sam Clayborne in the stomach.

Clayborne died in agony, writhing for minutes before his motion stilled, and it was characteristic of Bob Trask that he made no effort to help him, no real attempt to find out how seriously he was hurt.

He rose from the table, flipping the empty derringer to the floor. He wore a second gun in his holster at his hip, a forty-four. The noise in the hall had ceased. Men's faces were tilted up at the platform, frozen.

Trask's voice broke the tension. "You all saw it. He was going to shoot me."

There was no response.

Trask stood for a full minute, considering. Clayborne's death opened up new vistas before his eyes. He had no respect for the Judge and little for Sam's younger brother. They could never hold their mill and run the high-grading without Sam.

148

Once this was over, he would move in on their mill and organize the high-graders as they had never been organized before. There was only one person now in his way. Marc and Clint Hoe were dead. He did not know of Raoul's death, but he did not care. Raoul was of small importance either dead or alive. But he knew that one man stood between him and his actual control of the town. Les Hoe.

He lifted his voice then in a ringing challenge. "Come on, let's go over to the hotel and get the marshal from Deadwood. He started this, and it won't be finished as long as he's alive."

They stood aside to let him pass and then fell in behind him. The men he now led were a fairly disciplined crew. It was they who had been doing the stealing from the mine. He could be certain of most of them, but he could not be sure of the drunken crowd that filled the street.

Already some had forced their way into shops and were looting merrily. They broke off as Trask and his men appeared, and joined the marchers, carried forward by the crest of excitement. They came down the main street in a surging wave, swarming the sidewalks, working their way along the wagon-jammed street, calling, shouting, yelling.

Pierpont had placed his men well. Some were on the roof of the hotel, others at windows of the buildings across the street, but he had no illusion that his handful of company police stood any chance to halt this tide.

He and Lord Teal had stayed in the lobby, which was entirely deserted. The bar next door was closed, all lights extinguished, and on Pierpont's orders Sarah Baker had gone upstairs, but she had not gone to her room. Instead she lingered in the corridor, and she was standing there as Les Hoe came down slowly.

For a moment they looked at each other in silence. Then she said, in a voice still firm, without trace of fear, "What can I do, Les?"

He thought how different she was from any other woman he had known. Most women would be hysterical at a time like this. But there was no hysteria in Sarah. She was fully self-possessed. He said, "I just left Grandmére. I've been trying to get her to go. You might see what you can do. She likes and trusts you."

She nodded and moved toward the steps.

He said, "You can still get out the back way, and you've both got to get clear of the building. Everyone else has gone, and I wouldn't be surprised if they burn it."

She nodded again, and he went on down, to see Pierpont and Lord Teal beside the door, peering up the street.

The two turned as his boots sounded on the tiled floor, and the Englishman gave him a faint grin. "Excitement, what?"

He walked up to them. "What are you doing here?" He was speaking to Teal. "If I had a nice taproom to go to I'd have been headed that way an hour ago."

The man said a little ruefully, "Never did have much sense, you know. Wouldn't be in the bloody country if I did." He considered Hoe thoughtfully. "You know, wouldn't be too bad an idea if you took your own advice. You and Pierpont here, men they're looking for. Me, I can just get lost in the crowd when the shooting starts."

Pierpont said, "What are your plans? I've got men posted on the roof, more men at the windows across the street. We can probably drive them back. Most of them

150

are just full of liquor and spirits. They won't stay for too much when the rifles start cracking."

Les Hoe had a vision of the street being turned into bloody shambles. He shook his head. "I don't want to shoot down a bunch of hapless miners. Trask and Clayborne are the men responsible for this. I'm hoping they come first, that they'll walk in through this door where I'll have a chance to face them. Get word to your men not to start shooting until you give the signal." He broke off as a man came panting through the crowd and up the steps. It was Carl Henney.

"They're coming, thousands of them. Trask is leading them."

"Good." Hoe glanced at Pierpont. "You get into the barroom. I don't want them to see you when they march in. Tell your men across the street not to start shooting until you break the barroom window. Then tell them to fire twice over the crowd's heads. If they break and run, let them go."

"And how will I know when to break the window?" Pierpont's eyes were bleak. He did not approve. Pierpont, Hoe knew, was a good officer, but he had one thing in mind and one only, to enforce the law, and anyone or anything which stood in his way had to give.

Les Hoe had never approached the problem from quite the same angle. For violators he could be as ruthless as Pierpont, but he realized that often men were weak and unthinking rather than criminal.

He said, "Watch me through the door. If I go down, then let them cut loose."

He stood as Pierpont gave Henney the orders for the men outside the hotel, then saw the marshal fade through the connecting door into the dark barroom. Not until Pierpont had gone did he realize that Lord Teal still lingered in the lobby.

"You'd better get out of here."

Teal shrugged and hitched his gun belt around a little so that the walnut stock was in the proper place. "Always wanted to stand in a little fun. You watch yourself, Marshal. I'll watch your back."

He moved off, then, toward a far corner of the lobby beyond the desk and sat down easily in one of the leather chairs, as unconcerned as if he were a guest of the hotel and there was no trouble within a thousand miles.

Hoe admired the man's coolness, wondering how much of it was an act. Then he rounded the desk, sitting down quietly in the chair which the clerk sometimes occupied.

There was stillness in the empty lobby, stillness in the whole building. It was, he reflected, perhaps the first time since the hotel had been erected that it was entirely quiet.

And the silence of the interior was emphasized by the growing clamor from the street as Trask and his men moved deliberately forward.

They were within a quarter of a block, a hundred feet, fifty feet. Trask and those directly behind him were sharply alert, expecting trouble at any step. Nothing happened. There was no one on the hotel porch, and every window of the four-story structure was dark, save for the light which flooded out from the lobby lamps.

Trask's impulse was to halt. He sensed a trap. He had expected opposition before this, but the push of the crowd behind carried him forward almost against his will. He reached the hotel steps and mounted them, with as many of those as could pushing up after him through the wide doorway, and then he halted, irresolute.

At first glance he took the room to be empty, and his flashing thought was that Hoe had pulled out. Then he saw Teal in the corner and started, staring fixedly at the Englishman, who remained seated as if nothing out of the way had happened.

"What are you doing here?"

Lord Teal's cultured voice showed merely a hint of surprise. "And why shouldn't I be here, Mr. Mayor? This is a public place, and I find it restful after the turmoil of your streets. If you will permit me to say so, Your Honor, I don't think you have your town well in hand."

Trask's nerves were stretched near the breaking point. He had goaded himself to come here after Hoe, and he was suffering from reaction as the tension he had built up within himself eased.

"You damn renegade. Get out of here. If I see you in this town again I'll have you shot."

Edward Marmaduke Pemberton Teal, fifth son of an English baron, rose slowly, drew himself up to his full height. His eyes looked sleepy, his chin weaker than ever; his voice was soft, but it carried a bite, nevertheless. "Perhaps you had better start shooting, now."

Trask swore at him. He heard a snicker at his back, and as a politician he had a deep and abiding fear of ridicule.

"All right, you asked for it." He started to swing up the gun he had been holding loosely in his hand.

"I wouldn't." It was Les Hoe. He had risen quietly, unnoticed, from his place behind the desk, stepped to the chair, from it to the desk, and now he dropped lightly to the tiled floor, facing Trask, two-thirds of the length of the lobby separating them.

153

Trask was caught by surprise, quartered toward Hoe so that he would have to make nearly a half turn before he could bring his heavy gun to bear on the other man.

He stood helpless, undecided, his big body partly blocking the men in the doorway behind him. If he turned, Lord Teal would probably draw; if he fired at the Englishman first, he never questioned that Hoe would kill him.

His tongue moistened lips suddenly too dry, and he said in a strangled voice, "I'm here to arrest you for helping Shamus O'Shea escape from jail."

"And the men in the street?"

"They're my—my posse."

Hoe said, with a glint of hard amusement, "Rather a large posse for such a little chore, Mayor. I'm sorry, but I have to decline your invitation."

Trask licked his lips again. To have been so close to victory and then to have it snatched from his grasp! "You're through in this town, Hoe, you and your family. There are thousands of men out there in the street, just waiting to hang you."

Les Hoe's smile was wicked. "But that isn't going to do *you* any good, Trask. You're going to drop that gun, and then you're going to turn around, and with me behind you, you are going to step out onto that porch. You started this, and you're going to finish it. You're going to tell your men to go home. If they don't, you die."

Trask twisted his head, careful not to move his thick body, to give Hoe an excuse to shoot him. "You're bluffing. The minute you shot me they'd swarm into this building and drag you out and tear you limb from limb!"

"Maybe, but I've got a dozen good men covering the street from both sides. At the first sign of trouble they'll cut loose on the crowd. I'll take my chances. I don't think your mob would stand long in the face of concentrated fire. I'll take my chances."

"Don't be a fool." A harsh voice cut across the room, and he realized that Grandmére was on the stairs. "Shoot the dog down where he stands and then give the signal to cut loose on the crowd."

He did not turn. He kept his attention riveted on Trask, but she moved down until she was at his side, and he realized she was carrying a rifle. "If you haven't got the nerve, I have." The rifle came up to her shoulder, centering its sights on Trask's side.

CHAPTER 18

LES HOE'S HAND STREAKED OUT AND CAUGHT THE rifle, thrusting it upward as she squeezed the trigger. The sound of the shot brought a chain of action. Trask fired at Lord Teal, missing, and Teal missed two shots in return, for Trask had swung away and made a lunge for the safety of the doorway, pushing men out of his path in his wild dash.

There was a moment when Hoe could have shot him in the back. Instead Les used the instant to wrestle the rifle from Grandmére's grasp. He was still busy with her when a sickening crash burst from the barroom as the front window was smashed.

At once a rifle cracked from across the street, another, a third. Then as the mine guards steadied to their work, the shots took up an even rhythm.

Around Trask the street filled with startled, frightened cries. The mob which had swaggered confidently only moments before broke like so many panicked rabbits, diving for the first cover that offered.

A man beside Trask dropped, another threw up his hands, then doubled over to clutch his stomach and fall forward on his face. Trask's gun was still in his fist, and a great burning anger welled within him as he looked around for someone to shoot at. Hoe's guards were screened, their fire steady. Trask's army was melting away.

He turned and ran, a bullet smashing the window on his right. Whatever faults Bob Trask had, cowardice was not one of them, but he was not fool enough to fight a battle that was already lost. Not until he had covered three blocks did he stop, cursing himself for trying to attack Hoe on his own ground. He had been overconfident, but he was no longer deceived by the timbre of his followers. There were some twenty of them on whom he could depend. These were roughs who had run his assay offices, men he had brought to Two Mile for the sole purpose of helping him handle the stolen high-grade.

Of the general run of miners, only a few could be counted on to fight the Hoes. Drunk, excited, acting as a mob they would follow him as long as there was little or no real danger to themselves.

There had been nearly a thousand on the street as he led the march to the hotel. Now only his own men lingered, and even these showed decided signs of nervousness, as if they expected Lester Hoe and the mine guards to follow up their attack.

No, he should never have entered the hotel. He should have driven them out, with fire if necessary. That was it, fire. He could send a couple of men slipping down the alley. He turned and called to the closest.

"Two of you come here."

They walked up to him, uncertainly.

"Look," he said. "They shot us down like dogs. They think they've won, but there are other tricks in the game. Slip through to the alley and burn them out."

Both men were a little drunk. Both misunderstood, as Trask realized later, but then it was too late. He wanted them to burn the hotel. They thought he wished to burn the town, and they saw no reason for going as far south as the hotel to start the blaze. They chose the first saloon they came to. The room held a dozen customers, standing around nervously, waiting to see if Hoe and his guards were coming.

One of Trask's men leaped to the bar and, reaching upward, lifted down the big overhead lamp. Everyone watched him, startled, not understanding, until he dumped the oil into a trash container behind the counter. Then as he struck a match and tossed it into the oil-soaked paper, the horrified bartender grabbed up a bucket of water.

Trask's second man shot him twice, then drove the others from the saloon at the point of his gun. The fire licked up the flimsy side wall, spurting in little jets through the twisted cracks.

The original building was wrapped in flames, and its two neighboring structures already burning before Trask realized what had occurred.

Trask started to run down the block; then, sensing that it was fruitless to try to check the spreading flames, he stopped. He had seen other mining camps burn. Two Mile had a few stone buildings, but most of its structures were of wood, dry and tinderlike. With the strong downdraft from the peak above, it would be a matter of minutes only before the town was a holocaust.

He turned to his men, calling sharply, "Get what gold

and high-grade you have in the assay offices. Let's go up to the mine. We can watch the fire from there."

The cry of fire checked the stormy argument raging in the hotel lobby. At the first shots from his guards, Les Hoe had lifted his grandmother and pushed her behind the shelter of the hotel desk; then he ran into the dark barroom. Pierpont was at the shattered window, firing up the riotous street.

He caught the ex-marshal's arm angrily. "Why did you break the window?"

Pierpont said calmly, "I didn't. Someone outside threw a rock."

Les wasn't certain the man told the truth, but argument now was pointless. They both walked back into the lobby as the shooting died, and Grandmére rose to glare at Les across the desk.

"Is this the way you ran Deadwood? You had Trask. You'll never see a chance like that again."

He might have pointed out that the fault was hers. He didn't, for Sarah Baker was running down the stairs. "I tried to keep her out of the way."

"Never mind. Both of you have to get out of here before Trask rallies his men and tries again."

"I'll take them down to my place." It was Lord Teal.

Marie Hoe began to protest, but she was interrupted. "Fire," Carl Henney was shouting, racing up the steps, followed by several of the mine guards. "There's a fire in one of the buildings below the miners' hall."

"Fire." The most dreaded word in the mountain towns. An alarm bell rang from the far side of the canyon. A second answered it, then a third. Two Mile boasted three volunteer companies.

Les was already moving for the door. "We've got to clear the street. The engines have to get through."

His men followed, using their knives to slash the tangled harnesses which held the frightened horses and mules, pushing and pulling at the heavy wagons until a path was cleared through which the engines could make their way.

Hoe stood aside, wiping his forehead with the back of his hand. Then he turned to Pierpont as the volunteers snaked past. "We'd better check the men on the sidewalk." He indicated the half dozen still forms. "Some of them may be alive."

One was, and they carried him down to the doctor's office. Afterward they turned back up the street to where the engines were grouped, the volunteers running out their lines, starting to pump water from the creek and from the cisterns provided for the purpose.

The fire had already spread to a dozen buildings, and every few minutes another burst into blaze as the heat increased. The flames shot higher, and a fountain of sparks was driven before the wind.

A crowd had gathered. Many had been in the earlier mob, and their resentment and hate still rode them. "Let it burn. Let the Queen worry about it." They did not interfere with the fire fighters, but they offered no help.

And then O'Shea was suddenly there. Les did not know where he had come from, and, knowing the man's condition, he was surprised that he was able to walk.

Actually O'Shea had help, for Red Saunders was at his side, one big hand under the slighter man's arm, half supporting him, half carrying him.

Somehow O'Shea managed to clamber to the frame of the nearest engine, and anger made his voice ring clear above the murmur of the crowd, the crackling of the fire.

"What's the matter with you people? Why don't you

help fight the fire? This is your town. Everything you own is here, and to spite the Queen you'd stand aside and watch it burn. Think of your families, your homes, your children."

A small jeer answered. A voice called clearly: "They shot us down, the dirty scabs, the dirty murderers."

Red Saunders' bull-like voice cut back. "You all know me," he yelled. "Listen then, you drunken fools. There isn't a man alive I'm afraid to fight, and you can't say that anyone on this street ever stole more high-grade than I did."

A weak laugh rippled back at him, but his face was grim, red in the glow which made him look something like a devil.

"I tell you now I was a fool, just as you all were fools, playing Trask's game for him, lining his pockets while we ruined the mine that supports us, supports the town. Don't you have any pride? Don't you have the feeling that Two Mile belongs to you, that Two Mile is the best town in all of Colorado, the greatest town you or I will ever live to see?"

This time a cheer began, welling up until it seemed that everyone on the street was yelling.

"Save it then. When the fire is out, fight the Hoes if you want to. Take the town away from them, but don't destroy it. Two Mile is bigger than the Hoes, bigger than the union, bigger than all of us. Now, let's put our muscles on these pumps, let's throw more water than has ever been thrown in history."

He jumped down. He turned and helped O'Shea to the ground. A few men came off the sidewalk to grasp the pump handles; others followed, until the whole throng was milling forward, eager to help.

Saunders and O'Shea retreated to where Hoe stood,

and Saunders gave Les a fleeting grin. "Never knew I could orate."

O'Shea, gaunt as a scarecrow in the fierce, wrathful glow, said, "Someone get me a chair."

They broke the window of the nearest store and dragged an armchair to the sidewalk. The union man sank into it, his face twisting from the pain of his injured side.

"I'm taking over." He was talking to Hoe. "The union is running Two Mile until this fire is out."

Hoe did not answer, and O'Shea turned to stare at the fire. "What do you think, Red? Can they stop it?"

Saunders shook his head. Les Hoe agreed that it was hopeless.

"All right." O'Shea's voice rang with authority. "You're the best powderman in the mine. Take a dozen men who know what they're doing, go down to the powder sheds below the mill, and get what you need."

Hoe did not need to be told what was in O'Shea's mind. He'd seen dynamite used on boom-camp fires before. "Which block are you going to blow?"

O'Shea studied the onrushing flames, which were pushing the fire fighters steadily back. Then he turned, measuring distance.

"It will have to be the hotel block. They'd never get the charges set in time this side of it, with the rate the fire is traveling."

In spite of himself Hoe winced. The hotel, the bank building—two of the most impressive structures in Two Mile.

O'Shea had turned back, and his eyes bored into Les's face.

"It's up to you."

Les said steadily, "A moment ago you said you were

161

taking charge to save the town. Do what you have to do."

A smile broke across O'Shea's thin mouth. "You'll do to take along." It was high praise, coming from him. He looked at Pierpont. "Call up as many men as you need. Comb every street, knock on every door, warn them to get to the south end of town within ten minutes. Better if they are below the mill. There's going to be a lot of stone and timber flying through the air."

Pierpont nodded, hurrying away. The engines were again being moved back, driven from their positions by the increasing heat. The fire had now spread until it covered the full width of the gulch, a line with flames leaping into the air a hundred feet, sweeping onward as if nothing could halt it.

Hoe spoke to O'Shea. "There's nothing for me to do here. I'll go back and make certain the hotel is empty before the blasting starts." The sound of the fire was now so loud that he was forced to shout.

O'Shea did not trouble to answer, and Les turned, half running back along the street, to find Grandmére, Sarah, and Lord Teal in a tight group on the hotel steps. A band of refugees came hurrying by, carrying pitifully small bundles of possessions; and then he was surprised as Nell Clayborne moved out of the side street to join them.

Sarah had touched his arm. "How bad is it, Les?"

"Bad," he told her. "At the rate the fire is moving, it will be here in less than twenty minutes. Saunders is going to blow up this block, to try to make a firebreak wide enough so that they can check it and save the lower town."

Grandmére had been standing on the top step. She came down now to face him. "Blow up this block? You

162

mean the hotel?"

He nodded tiredly. He had expected this.

"They wouldn't dare."

He said quickly, "It's the only chance there is to save any of the town. Use your head. If the mill burns, the mine will be out of business for months. You know what that will mean."

"No. Whose idea was this?"

"O'Shea's."

"That radical. He'd love nothing better than to blow up my hotel."

He said. "I've no time to argue. O'Shea's trying to save the town, your town, can't you understand that?" She stared at him as if she had not heard the words

Suddenly she sprinted up the steps and stalked into the lobby. He was too surprised for a moment to move, then he ran after her, to find her seated in one of the leather chairs, her small hands folded primly in her lap.

"Go ahead. Let them blow it up. Blow me up at the same time. This is my monument, Les. Maybe you don't realize what that means. The day I finished this hotel, I was the most important woman in Colorado."

For an instant he felt helpless. Then, without argument, he scooped her up in his arms and carried her through the door. Lord Teal and Nell Clayborne stood, an uncertain pair, at the bottom of the steps.

Grandmére was fighting to free herself from his arms, and he looked around for Sarah for help. "Where's Miss Baker?"

"She went to make sure her husband was safe."

Les twisted to stare at Teal. "Her husband? Is he in Two Mile?"

The Englishman nodded. "I brought him up for her two months ago. I was going with her, but she said for

163

me to stay here, that you might need help."

"Where is he?"

"In that house which sets way up the canyonside, at the head of Moffet."

"Doesn't she know this whole block will go up in a matter of minutes? Here." He thrust Grandmére's small body into Teal's startled arms. "Take her down below the mill. Hit her on the head if you have to." He ran up Park as fast as he could, swearing under his breath as he ran, counting the minutes as he turned into Third and ran on toward Moffet. He knew that it would be close, very close indeed.

CHAPTER 19

THE STREETS THROUGH WHICH HE RAN WERE ALMOST deserted, for Pierpont's men had carried their warning to those householders who were not at the fire or who had not already deserted their homes.

The house he sought was not hard to find. It towered against the canyonside a good seventy feet above its fellows, its rear sill resting on a small shelflike depression in the almost vertical rock of the gulch wall, its front supported on long pine-pole stilts, its porch reached by a flight of steps which numbered nearly a hundred.

He raced up the steps. Sarah was not in sight, and although he shouted her name, there was no answer. At the top he paused for an instant to gain breath and, turning, had a full view of the fire, now alarmingly close. Then he ducked in through the open doorway to a hall whose only light was the glow from the raging flames below.

"Sarah."

There was silence, then her voice, calm, steady. "Up here, Les." And he was again running up steps, this time the narrow treads which led to the upper floor.

He found her in a small front bedroom, wrapping a blanket about the shoulders of a man who stirred listlessly under her efforts.

"Get out of here. Saunders will blow the block at any minute." He pushed her aside as he spoke and gathered up the man's spent body in his strong arms, hearing him murmur fretfully, "What is it? What's happening to me?"

"It's all right, Phil, all right." Sarah's voice was softer than Les had ever heard it, warmed by a maternal note. "Just relax. The town is on fire, but we'll get you out safely."

As he came down the narrow steps and out onto the porch Les had the time for a fleeting thought. This frail man, no good to himself or to anyone else, bound Sarah as securely as if she were tied. One misstep and she would be free.

But he did not pause. It seemed to him as he started down the long flight to the ground far below that the fire was hotter, that the flames were noticeably closer. He was a fourth of the way down, a half, and then the first blast burst beneath them, the second followed, then the third, and finally the fourth.

This house had not been mined, since it stood so far up the bank, but the earth trembled as if from a quake and the concussion knocked the stiltlike legs from under it.

Les Hoe fell backward against the steps and felt them crack and then give under him as the recurring blasts threw their mountain of shattered rock and timber high

165

into the air.

He never knew whether he had been struck on the head or had smashed his skull against the steps, but he blacked out and had no actual memory of falling.

Yet he was out so short a time that the last explosion still echoed from the far cliff and particles of broken boards still rained around him when he managed to sit up.

He was surprised to find that he still clutched Phil Baker's limp body in his grasp, that even in falling he had not released his hold. He sat up gingerly, relieved that although unconscious, the man in his arms was breathing weakly. And then he thought of Sarah, and panic came. The girl had been behind him on the steps, and her fall would have been longer than his.

He put Phil Baker down and struggled weakly through the wreckage of the splintered boards. Above him the house canted drunkenly, its front supports gone, held in place merely by the fastenings to its rear foundation. At any instant it might tumble down to crush them.

"Sarah." His voice was shrilly urgent. "Sarah, where are you?" And then he caught a glimpse of white on his left, and knew it was her shirtwaist, and pulled away the boards under which she lay.

She was breathing. He knew this much as he lifted her tenderly, seeing the blood from the cut on her high forehead and then he saw the left arm, which had been twisted grotesquely beneath her, and knew that the upper arm was broken.

Her eyes opened slowly, blurred, uncertain. Then memory came, and she struggled a little to get to her feet, still too numb to feel the pain from her arm.

"Les, you're all right?"

He had given no thought to himself. His arms and legs seemed to work properly.

"Fine," he said, without conviction.

"Phil? Where's Phil?"

He said gently, "He's all right. You've got a broken arm. How steady are you?"

She took a step and almost fell. He held her carefully "Stand still until I get your husband, then lean on me. We've got to get out of here before that house falls."

She glanced up quickly, but she showed no sign of panic. With all she had been through, Sarah Baker still had herself under full control.

He lifted the invalid as carefully as he could, and with her good hand grasping his shoulder for support, they picked their way down through the rubble that minutes before had been a solid, block-wide strip of buildings.

He was hardly conscious of the fire burning nearly to the line of wreckage, hardly conscious of the hundred small blazes set off in the rubble by the explosions.

Men were running forward, wetting down the devastated block, beating out the little blazes with shovels, with damp sacks, with anything that came to hand.

Someone saw them, and they were surrounded in a moment by an excited crowd. He knew vaguely when Phil Baker was taken from his arms, when the pressure of the girl's hand no longer clung tightly to his shoulder.

He was at the mill, and his grandmother was there, grim and silent, and Nell Clayborne threw her arms around him, clinging tightly, crying desperately with relief. He steadied her. The doctor had been looking after Baker in another room and was now setting Sarah's arm. He saw the girl wince with pain despite the shot of whisky the doctor had given her.

The mill looked like a hospital, for others had been hurt by the blast and in fighting the fire.

Nell's arms were tight about him as if she feared that he would vanish. He met Sarah's eyes across the other girl's shoulder, seeing them veil with a hurt that was deeper than the pain from her arm.

And then it was his turn. He sat in a chair in the office while the doctor patched a three-inch cut in his cheek and examined an ankle nearly twice natural size.

Hoe had not even been conscious of the ankle as he came off the canyonside. The door opened, and Lord Teal appeared. He looked at Les critically, as if to make sure he could stand news; then he spoke to the doctor.

"Better come. Miss Baker's husband is having a hemorrhage."

The doctor hurried out. Les followed as soon as he could work into his shoe. Phil Baker died before Hoe reached his side.

Teal had come out with him. He stood silent for a long minute as two of the doctor's volunteers carried the man's body away. Then he asked Les in a low voice, "Will you tell her, or shall I?"

Les Hoe hesitated, not wanting to see Sarah's face when she got the news. From behind, Nell Clayborne said, "I'll tell her," and he turned gratefully to watch the girl cross the big room. Suddenly the mill walls seemed to be closing in upon him. He had to get out, into the air, away from the injured, the scared, and the sick who filled the building. He hobbled out and started up the street toward the fire line. Half a dozen times during the four-block journey he was stopped by small squads of miners, placed at intervals to discourage looting.

It was daylight now, but you could not have guessed without the aid of a clock, for the heavy smoke which hung over the gulch completely blotted out all sign of the rising sun.

The main fire had reached the line of blasted buildings, and its tongues worked into the rubble, to be driven back by the constant spray of water pouring from the hoses. Behind the shattered block every roof held its quota of men, beating out sparks as they landed on the dry shakes or the sod, wetting down the surfaces with seemingly tireless bucket lines.

The miners had rallied. Once they had answered Saunders' appeal they had worked with a will. Blackened, weary, they still carried on, fighting to save what remained of the stricken town, and Hoe's heart warmed as he walked along the smoky street.

Towns have characters, each its own, built on the loyalty and strength of the men who live within its limits. He had known this in Deadwood, and he was learning it all over again here. Nothing bad could come out of a place like Two Mile, once its citizens were welded together by common service. O'Shea and Saunders had given them this night the kind of unselfish leadership which makes towns great. His grandmother and his brothers never had. They had been concerned only with building of brick and stone, not of men.

O'Shea still occupied his chair as if it were a throne and as if he truly was a descendant of the Irish kings. It had been moved back behind the line of the shattered block, but it was still the command post, the place where the weary workers came to receive further orders.

As Les reached his side, O'Shea said in a tired voice, "We've got her licked. When you want other towns blown up, send for Red."

Saunders grinned from beyond O'Shea's chair. "Powder goes off when you crimp the fuse right. It

169

don't matter much who lights the match."

Hoe noted the dark circles under the labor leader's deep-set eyes. "You'd better rest."

"Later." O'Shea's tone was short. "Too much to do. We've got women setting up kitchens at the lower end of town. We've sent to Denver for supplies and medicine. We've got over four thousand people homeless."

"You've done a wonderful job."

O'Shea looked surprised. "We've done little. It was the workers who turned out and helped. Remember that, when this is over."

"I'll remember." Les Hoe said this soberly. He watched the dying fire, the rolling, billowing clouds of smoke, then he went back toward the mill, meeting Nell on the street outside.

He said, "Did you tell Sarah about her husband?"

She nodded. Her blue eyes looked very large, very startled, as if they held unshed tears. "She's a wonder, Les. I couldn't take it as quietly if you were involved."

He understood.

"I almost died last night when you ran up the street after her and I knew there was a chance that you might not get out alive. I didn't know she had a husband. Lord Teal told me after you had gone. He explained how she has taken care of him for years."

He nodded.

"And I was surprised to find Mr. Teal such a gentleman. You hear so many wild stories about him."

Les Hoe was seeing Nell Clayborne in new perspective. He realized that most of his conception of the girl had been built upon his own fancy. Through the years he had drawn a mental picture of her, of how he wished she might be. She wasn't his picture.

170

There was nothing wrong with Nell Clayborne. She was good, loyal, honest, attractive, but although she would be a wife of whom any man might well be proud, he knew suddenly that he no longer had any desire to marry her, and yet, he had to marry her. It was so obviously what she expected, what she had a right to expect from his earlier manner, from the fact that she had compromised herself in coming to his hotel to warn him, in siding with him against her family—all little things, but threads which wove a pattern to hold him, even though his one dominating thought at the moment was that Sarah Baker was free.

He felt like a man in a trap. Why could not Sarah's husband have died while he and she were still in Deadwood, before he had seen Nell Clayborne again, before he had become involved with her?

"Sam's dead," she was telling him, and he realized that his mind had strayed, that she might have been talking for minutes without his hearing. "Clint shot him, and Clint's dead too. Did you know?"

He hadn't known.

"I feel lost without Sam. I seldom agreed with him, but he was the one I could turn to when I needed help."

She would always need someone to lean on; she lacked the hard core of strength that was Sarah's. He said, "You can be easy, Nell. Together we should face any situation."

Her hand tightened on his arm, and he knew now that she had had her moment of doubt, but that his words had reassured her.

They came into the mill together, and Lord Teal watched them from across the room with close attention. For three years the Englishman had watched Nell Clayborne, never approaching her because of the reputation he enjoyed in the country, being fully conscious that any approach by him would be misunderstood.

He saw the way she clutched Les Hoe's arm, and remembered the way she had acted on the night before when Hoe had left her to run after Sarah Baker, and his sandy brows straightened into a frown. He saw Hoe leave the girl to minister to some women and children at the lower end of the room, then move on into the mill office.

Edward Teal was not a man who usually busied himself in others' affairs, and he hesitated for a long minute before he followed.

"Talk to you for a minute?"

Hoe had crossed the office and was staring out of the window, so engrossed in his own thoughts that he had not heard the door open or close.

He turned, showing surprise. "Why not?"

Teal shifted uncertainly. "I'm about to do something I've never done in my life. I'm going to interfere in affairs that don't concern me."

Hoe saw that the Englishman was embarrassed. "What are you getting at?"

"I couldn't help but observe you coming in just now with Miss Clayborne."

Hoe stiffened a little. Lord Teal plunged on, looking thoroughly unhappy. "I also am not unaware of the talk that has been going on around Two Mile."

"What business is this of yours?"

"That's the point, old chap. It's not my business. But I'm making it mine." He looked more forlorn than ever. "Could I ask your intentions?"

Hoe laughed, in spite of himself. "Teal, this is Colorado, not England, but as it happens my intentions are the best. Nell and I are going to be married as soon as this mess is straightened out."

"A man is never happy living with the thought of two women."

Hoe was perfectly still. It ran through his mind that if anyone else had said this to him he might have shot him. Strangely, he was not angry with Teal. "What do you mean?"

"Bluntly, that you love Sarah Baker, and I have every reason to believe she loves you."

Here was the crux of Hoe's thoughts, put into words by someone else. He said shortly, "Sarah's strong. She will take care of herself."

"I wasn't thinking of Sarah." Teal's words came with painful effort. "I was thinking of Miss Nell. She's a fine woman. She deserves better than to marry someone who loves another woman."

"She'll never guess from any action of mine."

"I didn't mean that. I merely say that it isn't fair to her."

"In the love of heaven what do you want me to do? You are a gentleman. What else can I do?"

Teal's smile was wintry. "I was a gentleman once, and I don't know. But I still think it isn't fair. You might try telling her exactly how you feel."

"I can't," Les Hoe said. "I tried, but I couldn't." He turned and sat down heavily. Teal looked at him for a moment, then turned and quietly left the room.

CHAPTER 20

BY MIDAFTERNOON EVERYTHING NORTH OF PARK Street was tumbled ruin and smoldering ashes. The fire had ceased to blaze, but the tired crews still played their steady streams of water on the wreckage.

The smoky pall hung above the canyon, cutting out the sun. The town lay paralyzed, and a number of the homeless had already left, convinced that Two Mile was finished, that the destroyed portion of the town would never be rebuilt.

Les Hoe called a meeting of the labor leaders and as many of the merchants as could be located. Clint was dead. Raoul's body had been discovered beside the livery. Although the bank's stanch stone walls had resisted both the blast and the fire, the interior was ravished, and Les realized that all the records of both the mine and the bank were gone.

Who owned the bank? How much money had been on deposit? How much had the safe held? Did the bank have money on deposit with Denver and Eastern institutions? He did not know, but this uncertainty did not show in his manner as he faced the assembled men.

"We've all sustained a tremendous loss." His jaw was set, his eyes hard. "But we can't correct it by crying. The thing to do is start rebuilding. I'm sending a message to Denver this afternoon for all the lumber and supplies I can get."

There was a small cheer, but there was not much heart in it, and one portly man from the back of the room called, "It's all right for you Hoes. You have all the money in the world but what about the rest of us? How are we going to rebuild? How are we going to restock our stores?"

Hoe stared back at him. He did not know the man personally; perhaps he was one of those who had been willing to trade in high-grade, to help ruin the mine. That did not matter now. What mattered was the town. It

174

was strange. He had only been in Two Mile a few days, but suddenly he knew that it was his town, that he would do everything to make it live.

"As long as the Hoes have a dollar, as long as there is money or credit in the bank, as long as the mine can produce, we'll give credit to anyone who wants to rebuild, we'll back him for any goods he orders."

There was a cheer then. O'Shea jumped up from his seat in the front row. "The mine will be running tomorrow morning. The first shift will report on time and you can use a change room if you want, but I doubt it's necessary now. A man who would steal when the town needs the money is a dog."

The cheer grew. The spirit which Hoe and O'Shea had brought to the meeting filled them all and bound them together as nothing ever had before. They were a team. Les Hoe knew this as he returned to face his grandmother in the mill office; but he also knew that he still faced his hardest battle. Marie Hoe had quit.

She sat there, watching him as he talked, her eyes dull, her face nearly lifeless. When he finished she said slowly, "You've made big promises. How are you going to keep them? Where will you get the money to loan, let alone the money to rebuild our own property?"

"There has to be gold in the bank. As soon as the safe cools enough to open, we'll find out how much. The coins may be melted, but they are still gold."

"It doesn't belong to you or to me."

Hoe lost his temper. "What's the matter with you? You sent for me. You dragged me into this mess when you couldn't handle things yourself. Now you sit whining like an old woman merely because your precious hotel burned. Well, we'll build another hotel, twice as high, twice as fine."

175

"I still say what with?" Resentment was stirring in her voice, giving it more life.

"Look," he was standing over her now. "As far as anyone in this town suspects you're still the richest woman in Colorado. The records are all destroyed. We don't even know who the depositors are, or how many mortgages the bank held. And if we did know, what good would the knowledge be when the collateral is burned? This is a fresh start, Grandmére, a fresh start for you and for Two Mile, and as long as you hold your head high, as long as you act like the Queen, people will have no cause to doubt you. The mine opens tomorrow morning. Thank God, the mill still stands. We'll be running ore through here tomorrow night, all the ore that comes out of the ground, not just the low-grade which the miners didn't feel was worth stealing. In a month we'll have enough to pay off any depositor who can show his bank book. In two months this town will be back in business, better than it was."

She was watching him as if she had never seen him before. "Who's going to do all this? Marc's gone, Clint and Raoul are dead."

He said, "I can't prove it. Perhaps we'll never know for certain, but I think Clint bought your bank stock himself with the gold he stole from the mine."

She nodded slowly.

"If that's true, the bank still belongs to you. I hate to say it, Grandmére, but maybe the fire gave you another chance."

This was a new idea. He saw her consider it slowly. "But who's going to run all this?"

"You built the town once, you can build it again. You aren't so old."

Some of the former fire flashed in her eyes. "Who

176

says I'm old? But I need help. I had Marc before, and Clint, and even Raoul."

"I'm here."

"One man can't do it all."

He thought of O'Shea and dismissed the thought. O'Shea's real interest was not building businesses. It was in strengthening labor. He sensed that a strong union, well run, was as good for industry as it was for labor, but no one man could handle both jobs objectively.

He thought of Pierpont, but the marshal lacked training and imagination, and then he thought of the Englishman.

"Lord Teal."

He saw the protest form on her lips and stopped it with a gesture. "Use your head. Stop being an opinionated woman. Teal stood by last night when we needed him. He's better educated than anyone else in Two Mile and he's my friend."

She said slowly, "You're making the decisions."

"I am," he said. "But you have to give the over-all orders. Without your guidance I couldn't rebuild the town."

Her lips pursed. He noticed that her shoulders, which had been bowed when he first came in, had straightened, and he thought, "I've won." She had quit, but she was back on the track now. Another minute and she'd be giving orders in the same old way, perhaps threatening him with her whip.

He grinned. It had hurt him, deep down inside, to see her quit. Never before had he realized quite how much she had meant to him, how much she had steered his development. She had been the only family he could remember, and her very stubbornness had built up his own.

"I'd better call Teal before you change your mind." He walked to the door and told one of the men in the outer room to find the Englishman and send him to the office. Then he turned back to find that his grandmother had already picked up a pen and was making a list of figures.

She stopped suddenly. "Les, did you come in here purposely to make me mad, to get me going again?"

He nodded.

"You're smarter than I thought, but there's one place that you aren't smart at all."

"What's that?"

"Sarah Baker. I talked to her before you got back. She's leaving town on the first stage unless you stop her."

The news came as a shock, although he had expected it. But he managed to control his voice as he said, "And how do you think I could stop her?"

"Marry her, you fool. She has the crazy notion that you love Nell Clayborne."

This hurt bitterly, but he still managed to mask his feelings, saying, in a steady voice, "Crazy or no, I'm marrying Nell as soon as this mess is straightened out."

"Fiddlesticks." The word coming from his grandmother sounded like an oath. "You don't want to marry her and you know it."

"You're wrong." His voice was steady. "I wonder if you realize how much I owe to Nell?"

"Because she was fool enough to come to your hotel room and start the town gossiping about her?"

"Because she is who she is, what she is. All my life, everything I've done, has been in an effort to make myself good enough for her. It's what kept me going, probably what kept me on the right side of the law."

"Good enough for her." The words were a snort. "I'll show you who's good enough for who." She came out of her chair and strode across the office to pull open the door, entirely herself again, now that there was a crisis to meet.

The crowd of refugees at the far end of the big mill stirred as she came toward them, her sharp eyes spotting Asa Clayborne and his daughter in a small group beside the settling tanks.

"Judge, you and Nell come into my office."

Clayborne stood up in surprise. It was the first time in nearly fifty years that Marie Hoe had spoken to him directly. Nell had risen also, her face going white, then coloring as she guessed that Les must have told the Queen of their coming marriage.

Silently they followed Marie Hoe back into the office. Deliberately she shut the door and then walked to the desk. Nell moved to Les's side, as if needing his protection, and Marie Hoe considered them all with baleful eyes.

"Asa, these two want to get married."

The Judge started.

"Are you going to tell them why they can't or shall I?"

Scarlet rose into Clayborne's face, and he shifted uneasily from one big foot to the other. When he spoke his tone lacked its usual strength. "I guess maybe you'd better tell them, Marie."

It was at that moment that the door behind them was pushed open and Lord Teal stepped into the room. He started to say, "You sent for me," but didn't, for Grandmére was already talking.

"You can't marry her," Grandmére's voice was low,

"because she is your aunt. She is your father's half sister."

For a moment the room was utterly quiet, then a single word burst from Nell. "No."

"Yes." Marie Hoe's voice grew grim as she indicated Clayborne with a motion of her head. "When he was a young man he made a trip to the country south of New Orleans and met me. I was fifteen at the time, and I believed him when he said he would marry me. But instead he went back north to the Cape, and when I found I was to have a baby I followed him."

Clayborne spoke desperately. "I went north to tell my family. I was coming back. You shouldn't have followed. You ruined everything by talking to my father."

Grandmére's old lips curled. "You were always weak, Asa. I didn't realize that then, that other people would always do your thinking."

Les said sharply, "Why didn't you tell us this before?"

Her voice was still grim. "Because I made a promise. I came north to the Cape, and I talked to Asa's parents, and they refused to believe that the child belonged to their son. However, they offered me enough money to get along in return for the promise that I would never speak to Asa again and that I would tell no one who the boy's father was. I was a thousand miles from home, friendless. I had little choice. I promised. But I also made myself a vow that no matter what he did or where he went I would hound Asa Clayborne for the rest of his life." To Les her words explained many things which had long puzzled him; but she was not quite finished.

"My boy grew up. He married young. His wife died when Les was born. Never knew he was a Clayborne. I

180

told him he was Cajun, like myself, his father a riverman, killed in a boat explosion. Then the war came, and he was killed at Shiloh, leaving me with his four small boys to raise. I almost went to the Judge for help then."

Clayborne's tone was hoarse. "I wish you had. I always have loved you very much." He sank into the chair beside the desk as if he lacked the strength to stand.

"I loved you, too." Her voice was relentless. "But hate and love are not too far apart, and I come of a race that hates well. You'd married by that time, and had other children, and I set myself to ruin you, to drive you from the Cape. I did, and then I followed, one state to another, one camp to the next. And you never fought back until we reached Two Mile. I would have respected you more if you had."

Clayborne bowed his head under the weight of her words. Les said, "Well, I—"

Nell interrupted. "Please." She had freed the arm he had been holding and turned quickly toward the door. Not until that moment did she see Teal, standing uncomfortably before her.

Edward Teal would have given everything he had ever owned not to have been present during that moment. He had stood rooted during Grandmére's words, not wanting to attract attention to his presence by any movement, hoping desperately that the opportunity would offer itself for him to slip unseen back through the doorway.

But the chance had not come, and now his full concern was for the girl, realizing the shock the words had been to her.

"Miss Nell, I—"

"Take me out of here, please."

At once he offered his arm. Ten generations of Teals had been aristocrats, and manners are an inherent thing. She walked out on his arm, her head held high.

Les watched after them, then turned to his grandmother. She had moved around the corner of the desk, had put one small hand on Clayborne's bent shoulder. Both of them were crying quietly.

He walked slowly from the room, crossed the mill, and stepped out into the roadway. A stage was loading a group of refugees. Even as he emerged the driver raised his whip, spoke to his horses, and the heavy vehicle lumbered into motion. As it passed, Les Hoe caught a glimpse of Sarah Baker's face through the window.

He shouted, but it was too late, for the stage was already gathering momentum as it headed downgrade, the horses at a half run.

He looked after it a long minute, then turned, racing back to the livery for a horse.

CHAPTER 21

BOB TRASK HAD WATCHED THE FIRE FROM THE BREAST of the mine dump. Long before the flames were extinguished he and the twenty men with him had decided that Two Mile was finished, that the town would never rise again.

Trask made his plans accordingly. They would leave the gulch as soon as possible, but not one of them had any notion of leaving empty-handed. The town, for all it lay a waste of ashes, still held gold in large quantities, and they meant to take as much of the money with them as possible.

The bank was their first thought, but Trask recalled that the town-hall safe held the bond money which Sarah Baker had put up for Les Hoe's release, and that each of the assay offices scattered throughout town had its supply of gold.

There were three light buckboards at the mine, which had been used for gold shipments, and horses in the stable below the dump. An hour after nightfall they harnessed the teams and drove slowly down the mountainside into the area laid waste by fire.

They met only slight trouble, with three men whom O'Shea had posted to prevent looting. These they disposed of silently, effectively; then they moved on to the ruin of the city hall.

From the safe they removed Sarah Baker's money, run together by the intense heat until each bag of gold coins had become a misshapen lump. Then the main group of Trask's men moved on down to the bank while others went to the assay offices to clean out their safes.

Once inside the bank, Trask expected trouble with the safe. As mayor, he had known the combination of the city-hall safe, and of course the combinations of the safes in his various assay offices, but the bank was a different proposition.

The roof and windows were gone, the interior gutted, but the stout stone walls had withstood even the force of the explosions. The ashes were still so hot that the men could feel the heat through the soles of their boots, and the safe, which had fallen onto its face from the force of the blasts, blistered their palms as a dozen of them grabbed it and rocked it back onto its wheels.

As they did so, the unlocked door swung open and the contents fell out. Here, too, the heat had partly melted the coins, fusing them together into uneven lumps. These the men seized eagerly, although they were still hot enough to sear the skin, and in slings made of their coats they carried them out to the buckboards.

They worked over an hour, loading the gold from the bank, from the assay offices, and from small safes in the surrounding stores. They worked undisturbed, for the exhausted town slept, packed in the buildings south of Park.

They might have gotten entirely free of the town without being observed had not O'Shea, sleeping on a cot in the mill, stirred. He lay for a moment, quietly, then he sat up and lit a match to examine his watch.

The three men he had put on patrol were supposed to work only a two-hour shift, then come and wake him so that he could substitute fresh watchers.

He rose and, moving to the next cot, shook Red Saunders awake.

The redhead sat up, rubbing his eyes. "What's the matter?"

"It's four hours since the patrol went out. We'd better check. Something's wrong."

"Go back to sleep." Saunders stood up and stretched. "I'll take a look."

O'Shea was stubborn. "I'll go with you." Together they threaded between the rows of exhausted men sleeping on the floor, out into the darkness.

The smell of burned wood lingered heavily in the air, and a hush hung over the gulch in strange contrast to the raging sound which had filled the streets the night before.

They stood, peering northward in the darkness toward the burned-over section, and then they heard noise. Without a word they turned and headed east along the cross street, coming out just short of the livery, pausing as they saw the bobbing light of a dozen lanterns. Men moved in and out of the wide runway.

Trask's men were after mounts, saddling one horse and then another, tying them to the rail beside the barn.

O'Shea pushed forward, seeing the three rigs, recognizing Trask's heavy figure as the mayor came out leading another horse.

"Trask."

Bob Trask stopped. He knew the voice, and his heavy lips flattened a little against his teeth.

"What do you think you're doing?" O'Shea had come into the circle of light thrown by the lanterns, followed by Red Saunders.

Trask eyed him, debating. He had hoped to get out of Two Mile unobserved. The last thing he wanted was to arouse the town.

He schooled his voice to sound reasonable. "We're pulling out. Two Mile is through. We don't want trouble. We just want to go."

"What's in the buckboards?"

Trask hesitated. "Just the gold from my assay offices. A man's got a right to take his gold with him, hasn't he?"

O'Shea walked to the wagons, noting the irregular lumps of half-melted coins. "All from your office?" He swung around. "From the bank, I'd guess, and a lot of other places." His hand dropped to his gun.

Trask shot him twice, cursing as he did so. Red Saunders saw O'Shea crumple and fall and, with a yell that was not quite human, he charged directly at Trask.

The gun in the mayor's hand exploded, the heavy bullet knocking Saunders half around and dropping him to his knees. Saunders struggled upward, and the horse which Trask had been leading swung away, loose, startled by the shots. As he passed, Saunders grasped the saddle's horn and managed to swing himself onto the frightened animal's back.

Trask shot after him twice, one bullet missing, the second nicking the horse. The animal was definitely running away, thundering down the grade toward the trail which led to Teal's.

Trask swore. "One of you catch him. We don't want a witness to O'Shea's death."

Two of his men jumped for horses and went pounding after Saunders. Trask turned as the rest ran from the barn "Let's get out of here before the whole town comes alive." He swung into his saddle, listening for a shot that would tell him Saunders was silenced forever. He did not hear it.

Saunders was clinging to the horse desperately as the animal cut down the slanting switchbacks of the trail. He could hear the pound of hoofs and knew that his pursuers were not far behind. The bullet had struck his right side, and he had difficultly using it.

Had it not been for his enormous strength and the long legs locked firmly around the horse's belly, he would never have managed to keep his seat.

His side was numb, his shirt sticky with blood. He had no idea how much blood he had lost. He was a little lightheaded, but he could still hear the sound of the men behind him. Teal's was the first possible place where he might get help, and he had no idea whether anyone save the Indian hostlers would be there. But at least there was a light when he drove his now staggering horse into the wide meadow and pulled up before the corral fence.

Les Hoe and Sarah Baker heard him ride up and paid no attention. For two hours they had been sitting in the inn's big front room, talking quietly.

186

Les had caught the stage at Teal's. When he pulled open the door, the girl stared at him in surprise. "Les, what are you doing here?"

His face was grim. "So you were running out without even saying good-by?"

"It seemed the best way." Her voice was low. "The easiest way."

He took her arm, leading her out of the hearing of the other passengers.

"Why, because of Nell?"

She nodded silently.

He told her then, repeating his grandmother's words as nearly as he could.

She caught her breath when he reached the end, when he told her that he had left Grandmére and the Judge alone in the office, both in tears.

"Les, I'm terribly sorry for them, the wasted years."

He said, "And yet you and I were both willing to waste our own chance."

After the stage left, they sat talking, really alone for the first time in their lives, not conscious of the passage of time until they heard Saunders' horse, heard the man's heavy dragging steps on the porch, and then saw him half fall into the room.

"Hoe." It was a gasp of relief. This was far better luck than Saunders had expected. "They'll be here any minute." He sank into a chair.

"Who?" Hoe jumped to his feet.

"Trask, and about twenty men. They killed O'Shea, and they've been chasing me."

"Killed O'Shea?"

"Yes. They looted the bank and I don't know how much else. They've got three buckboards loaded with

187

gold."

Hoe thought of his plans to rebuild the town, of the thousands of people who would be uprooted, ruined, if Two Mile did not grow again. The gold in the bank must not be lost.

"How many men are here?"

"Only Teal's Indian boys—three I think."

The redhead groaned. Sarah said sharply, "You can't stop twenty men, Les. You'll be killed, and for what? Let them have the gold."

He looked at her, remembering that she had stripped herself of everything she had to go his bond and that she had left Two Mile, never giving the money a second thought. He started to explain, but the drum of hoofs around the upper bend above the meadow broke his words.

He turned, glancing around, spotting Teal's heavy rifle with its belt of shells hanging from the antlers above the fireplace.

He grabbed it, calling to the girl to get out of sight and stay there; then he ran into the yard, loading the rifle as he ran.

The noise from the trail above him increased steadily. He ran past the corral fence, finding a shelter in a small pile of rock not far from the canyon wall.

Here he pulled up, waiting until two horsemen swept around the bend. He could see them outlined in the half light from a sickle moon. He saw them spot Saunders' weary animal near the fence and swerve toward it, yelling at each other as they came. They hauled up, swinging to the ground, and stood for a moment looking at the horse. In that instant Les stepped around the rocks, his rifle ready.

"All right, get your hands in the air."

One of the men spun about, sending a quick shot over Les's head, and Hoe shot him, coolly, deliberately.

As he dropped, the second man dived through the fence, trying to get the horses between himself and Hoe, shooting wildly. He did not see Red Saunders come out of the inn's rear door, steady himself against the wall, draw the heavy revolver with his left hand, and calmly shoot him in the back of the head.

For a long minute the yard seemed very quiet after the explosions of the heavy arms; then they caught the sound of the rest of Trask's party on the trail above them. Saunders' voice came across the darkness.

"The next won't be so easy, Marshal. Maybe you and the girl should get some horses and ride for it."

"And let Trask get away? No, thanks."

"I didn't think you would." Saunders' voice held a certain satisfaction. "Any man who can lick me wouldn't run from anything." He took one step away from the wall and then, to Les Hoe's horror, his legs collapsed under him and he fell to the ground.

Hoe ran forward to bend over him. The big redhead had lost too much blood. He was out cold. Hoe turned, listening to the oncoming riders, then stooped and lifted Saunders in his arms.

He staggered under the two hundred and twenty pound load as he carried it up the steps and into the kitchen. Sarah Baker opened the door for him. She had found a shotgun and was carrying it in the crook of her arm.

He said tensely, "They'll be here in less than five minutes. There are three saddled horses at the fence. Get one, ride down canyon."

"Not unless you come with me."

He jerked his head at the unconscious Saunders,

whom he still held. "If I leave they'll kill him, first thing."

"I didn't expect you to leave." She was, he realized, perfectly calm, utterly unafraid. The fact that eighteen murderers with nearly a half million dollars' worth of gold were riding down upon them did not affect her any more than someone winning a split on the faro bank.

"You're wonderful," he said. "Where will I hide him?"

"The bar."

"Probably the first place they'll break into if they down us."

"There are rooms upstairs."

He carried Saunders up the narrow twisting stairway that led from the kitchen, placing the injured man gently on a lumpy bed.

He turned then, running down the steps as he heard Trask's party swing into the yard and pull up beside the corral.

Peering from the kitchen doorway, he made out the outlines of the three buckboards, the shadowy figures of the men as they swung out of their saddles. He heard their curses as they straightened from examining the dead men beside the fence and heard Trask's voice ring out through the night

"Saunders got both of them."

"He had help." Hoe stepped around the corner of the house, his rifle held ready. "I want you, Trask. The rest of you mount up and get out."

Someone in the crowd snapped a shot at him. He fired twice in return before jumping back to the shelter of the house, and continued on, running across the slope of the meadow as it rose to meet the canyon wall.

They boiled around the corner of the house, and he

purposely fired into the air, to draw them away from the house, away from the girl and the wounded man.

He heard the snap of their short guns. He was not too worried. At this range if anyone hit him with a revolver it would be sheer accident.

They were running after him, spreading but in a kind of skirmish line. By the time he reached the timber, bullets searched after him, screeching through the pine and aspen to splatter against the rocks.

He climbed. He had no set plan in mind. He only knew that one man in timber under the cover of darkness had a definite advantage. Every movement he heard would mean an enemy, while Trask's men could not be certain that they were not shooting at each other.

Trask had sense enough to know this too. Trask called a halt. He kept four men with him, split the others into two parties, sending one up canyon, one down.

The plan was perfectly clear to Hoe. They would climb the canyon on either side of him, then at daylight work downward, forcing him into the open.

He could beat them over the rim and thus escape the jaws of their trap. But he would be afoot in broken country, cut off from the inn.

He held his place, watching the men still in the meadow below him, wishing they would come a little closer. They were out of rifle range.

Suddenly there was a diversion from the inn. He heard the sound of a running team, a second, then a third. Trask also heard the horses. He turned, shouting, and with his men ran back toward the buildings.

Hoe went after them. He ran, ignoring the pain which shot up from his swollen ankle. He had covered half the distance when a shotgun's blast rocked the night. There was a long high cry before he burst around the building

191

corner. Trask was struggling with the girl, who, hindered by her broken arm, was making a poor fight of it. Trask's men, already mounted, were heading down canyon at a wild run. The buckboards had vanished.

Trask heard Hoe and spun around, holding the girl as a shield, lifting his heavy gun. But the bullet buried itself in the dirt at Les Hoe's feet, for Sarah had thrown her full weight against his arm.

Hoe jumped in, grabbed Trask's wrist, wrenched the weapon free. The girl stumbled to the ground, and Trask swung heavily, burying his big fist in Hoe's side, knocking the wind from the body of the lighter man.

Hoe fell against him, locked his arms around the thick neck as he struggled for air, and managed to knock Trask's feet out from under him. They fell. Trask rolled, trying to get on top. Hoe was still short of air. He felt the man's heavy body upon him, fingers gripping his throat, and through a daze he heard the girl's warning yell.

"Knife, he's got a knife."

Trask had used his free right hand to pull a knife from his belt, and his arm swung up. Hoe somehow broke the grip at his throat, to reach up and catch the heavy wrist, pushing it away with all his strength.

Trask tried to wrench loose, and Hoe rolled, trying to drop the heft of his body against the arm. Instead he lost his grip, but did manage to roll free. They gained their feet almost at the same instant, circled, like two fighting bears, looking for an opening.

Hoe charged suddenly like a striking cat, snatching at the wrist with his right hand. He missed, and the thick blade slashed his forearm to the bone. But before Trask could free the knife, the fingers of Hoe's left hand closed like iron bands around the wrist. He twisted his

192

body, bringing the extended arm up over his shoulder, his whole weight a lever which catapulted Trask into the air.

The man fell curled up, his arms under him. Les Hoe used his feet to jump on his back, to drive the air out of him; fell forward and wrapped his good arm around the thick neck. Not until then did he realize that Trask was not resisting, that he was utterly motionless.

Slowly he straightened, expecting a trick, but Trask still made no motion, and gingerly Hoe turned him over. Trask had fallen directly on the point of his own knife, his momentum driving it deep into his chest. He was dead.

Hoe stood panting in the thin air. His right arm hung useless at his side. The girl ran to him, lifting the arm in her good hand, staring at the blood which bubbled from the cut. "You've got to have a tourniquet." She lifted her dress and caught her petticoat, trying to tear it free, hampered by her own useless arm.

Hoe came to her aid. He nearly jerked her from her feet as he ripped the underskirt free of her long, straight legs.

Together they ripped it into strips and fashioned a bandage around his upper arm. She found a stick and twisted it until the flow of blood was stopped.

He kissed her then, holding her for a long moment, feeling her body tremble against him.

"What happened to the buckboards?"

She said, "I figured Trask wanted the gold more than he wanted you. I spooked the teams, and he came running back. I missed him with the shotgun. I'm not so good, using one arm."

He said, "Better get it and reload." He caught up his rifle from the ground and ran to the corner of the house.

In the growing half light of coming dawn, Trask's men, who had climbed into the brush, were trotting across the meadow to the inn.

He raised his rifle with his left hand, steadying it against the log corner of the building, and fired.

They stopped uncertainly, and in the following silence his ear picked up the sound of horses rushing down the canyon from above. He turned, almost sick with reaction and weakness as he watched them stream into the yard, Pierpont in the lead.

"Hoe." The marshal swung down beside him in surprise. "Have you seen Trask, a bunch of men, and three buckboards?"

Hoe gestured with the rise toward where Trask still lay beside the corral fence. "Part of his men are in the meadow behind the inn or in the brush of the canyonside. Four of them rode after the buckboards. Sarah spooked the teams and they ran away. How'd you happen to get here?"

"The hostler at the livery. He was sleeping in the hay when Trask broke into the barn after horses and he stayed quiet, but he heard about the gold, and when they left he found O'Shea's body."

Pierpont turned, ordering half a dozen of his men down canyon after the buckboards, the rest to search the meadow and guard the inn. Then he, too, rode after the gold.

A doctor had come down with the posse. He sewed up Les's arm, readjusted Sarah's splints, which had slipped during her struggle with Trask, and then climbed the stairs to examine Red Saunders, whom he pronounced out of danger.

It was almost noon before Pierpont rode back with two prisoners and the banged-up buckboards. "They weren't coming back," he reported. "They were heading out of the country." The other two men were dead, but with the men who had been flushed out of the brush beyond the meadow they had eight prisoners.

Les went into the inn, where Sarah was relieving the doctor at Saunders' bedside, and motioned her into the hall. "Pierpont's back. It's time to ride for Two Mile."

"Do you want to go?"

He was startled. "Go, but of course I want to go. There's a town to rebuild, a mine to reopen."

Her hand closed on his good arm. "Les, I know your grandmother, and so do you. She'll rebuild the town and you'll wind up doing nothing but taking orders, running her errands. It's her town, not yours, and it will be that way as long as she lives."

"I don't think so. I think she's really learned a lesson out of all this."

"And if we go back, you will always be Les Hoe, ex-marshal of Deadwood, and I'll be Sarah Baker, the woman who ran a gambling saloon. Can't we go someplace else, someplace where people know nothing about us, where we can change our names and live our life quietly?"

She saw the stubborn set of his mouth and thought, "He doesn't want to do it," and her tone changed. "All right, Les. I'll go any place you want to go, do anything you want to do." She held up her mouth for his kiss.

They rode in one of the buckboards up canyon, drawn by fresh horses from Teal's stable, and their arrival at the mill was a kind of triumph. It seemed that the whole remaining population of Two Mile had gathered there in the street.

Somehow Les forced an opening through the cheering crowd. He did not see Grandmére and asked the mill

195

foreman where she was. The man jerked his head toward the office, and, with Sarah holding his arm, he crossed and gently pushed open the door.

Grandmére and Asa Clayborne sat side by side at the big desk, examining a sketch that the woman was drawing, oblivious of the excitement in the street outside. Les and Sarah stopped, knowing that they were unobserved, and heard Grandmére say, "We'll move the bar over here, the dining room is here, the kitchen in the ell., and in this corner we'll have a women's parlor so that they won't have to wait in the main lobby."

She looked up, then, and saw them, and said, "Good work. Pierpont sent a rider up to tell us you'd gotten back the gold."

Les stared at her. He had expected more emotion.

"We've got the hotel plans drawn. I'll have the builder make up a materials list. You can take it to Denver and fill it. Then as soon as you come back you can start on the bank, and afterwards—"

Les stopped her then. "Wait a minute, Grandmére. Someone else will have to do it. Sarah and I are going away."

"Away? You can take her with you to Denver. It will serve as a wedding trip."

"Away," he corrected her. "For good. We've got our own life to live. I was wrong. I thought rebuilding Two Mile was the most important thing in the world. It isn't, not for us."

Her old eyes hardened. "So, you're running out on me again, just when I need you. Well, if you leave me now, this is the end. You'll not see a nickel of my money, not a single nickel."

Surprisingly Asa Clayborne spoke harshly. "Shut up, Marie."

196

She turned on him, almost savagely, but he did not quail. "Let the children alone. This isn't their problem. It's ours. We can build the town together without their help."

Her mouth opened and closed twice; then she said in a different tone, "Come here, Sarah."

Sarah went forward slowly. Marie Hoe stood up. She put both her hands on the girl's shoulders and kissed her on both cheeks. "Take care of him. Someday he'll have to come back and run this. But build your life. It's a good thing to have someone to work with." She dropped her hands then, and one of them slid into Clayborne's broad palm.

Outside in the big room Sarah was near tears. "I feel bad, Les, taking you away. They need you. They're old."

He said, "They don't need me. I'd just be in the way, and they're not too old for the job. I guess you're never too old when you're pioneers."

We hope that you enjoyed reading this
Sagebrush Large Print Western.
If you would like to read more Sagebrush titles,
ask your librarian or contact the Publishers:

United States and Canada

Thomas T. Beeler, *Publisher*
Post Office Box 659
Hampton Falls, New Hampshire 03844-0659
(800) 251-8726

United Kingdom, Eire, and
the Republic of South Africa

Isis Publishing Ltd
7 Centremead
Osney Mead
Oxford OX2 0ES England
(01865) 250333

Australia and New Zealand

Australian Large Print Audio & Video P/L
17 Møhr Street
Tullamarine, Victoria, 3043, Australia
1 800 335 364